THE ENIGMATIC
GREEK

THE ENIGMATIC GREEK

BY

CATHERINE GEORGE

MILLS
BOON

First published in Great Britain 2013
by Mills & Boon, an imprint of Harlequin (UK) Limited.
Large Print edition 2013
Harlequin (UK) Limited, Eton House,
18-24 Paradise Road, Richmond, Surrey TW9 1SR

© Catherine George 2013

ISBN: 978 0 263 23189 2

Harlequin (UK) policy is to use papers that are natural,
renewable and recyclable products and made from
wood grown in sustainable forests. The logging and
manufacturing process conform to the legal environmental
regulations of the country of origin.

Printed and bound in Great Britain
by CPI Antony Rowe, Chippenham, Wiltshire

With love and thanks to *my* Alex.

CHAPTER ONE

His island had lain in the sun in this remote part of the Aegean Sea long before Bronze Age Minoans had sought refuge here from cataclysmic disaster on Crete. Normally Alexei Drakos relished its peace. Today, not so much. From his office in the *Kastro* he gazed down, frowning, and then abandoned the view of brilliant blue sea lapping at the golden beach far below to make a comprehensive check of the banks of technology across the room. But for once they failed to hold his attention. Feeling restless, and plagued by something unfamiliar he refused to identify as loneliness, he turned back to the windows to watch a ferry in the distance discharging its cargo of holiday-makers into the *tavernas* lining the harbour of the neighbouring island.

Tomorrow tourists like these would flock here to his island for *Agios Ioannis.* Bonfires would blaze on the beaches to celebrate the feast of

St John and visitors would come in droves for the festival and for the highlight of its entertainment, the bull dance famed for origins which reached far back into antiquity. Those Minoans again. But it was worth the sacrifice of privacy for a single day. The islanders who made a living from fishing here on Kyrkiros had reaped big benefits from his decision to revive the festival. It brought tourists who paid them an entrance fee, ate their food and bought their crafts, sampled their olives and honey, drank the wine from the island vineyards and ordered more from the websites he'd set up. But otherwise left the island in peace.

Suddenly tired of his own company, he made the descent by the ancient, winding stairs for once to burn off some of the energy buzzing through his system and entered the big, modernised kitchen on the ground floor of the *Kastro* to exclamations of pleasure from the women working there.

'You should have rung, *kyrie*,' scolded his housekeeper, pouring coffee. 'I would have come up to you.'

He shook his head as he took one of the pastries she offered. 'I knew you would be busy, Sofia.'

The woman smiled fondly. 'Never too busy to

serve you, *kyrie*. And nearly all is ready now for tomorrow. A good meal is prepared for the dancers, and Angela and her daughters have done marvels.'

'They always do.' He smiled at the women who every year fashioned traditional costumes based on designs discovered on ancient, barely discernible frescoes during the *Kastro's* restoration.

Sofia smiled lovingly as her son came hurrying in. 'Is all in place, Yannis?'

The youth nodded eagerly. 'You wish to check, *kyrie*?'

Alex downed his coffee and stood up. 'Lead on.'

In contrast to the normal peace of the island, colourful stalls had been set up on the sweep of beach below. Higher up, on the natural shelf overlooking the terrace where the dancers would perform, a vine-wreathed pergola sheltered tables reserved in advance by the forward-thinking of the influx of visitors expected the next day. He nodded in approval to the men finishing up there. 'Well done, everyone.' With a reminder to check that all the necessary signs were in place, he returned to his office, but this time via the lift he'd installed years before as one of the first steps towards making the *Kastro* penthouse habitable. His phone rang as the doors opened and he smiled as he saw the caller ID.

'Darling,' said a lilting, unmistakeable voice. 'I'm tired and thirsty and I've just landed at your jetty.'

His eyebrows shot to his hair. '*What?* Stay right there. I'm on my way.'

The moment the lift hit ground level again, he raced out of the *Kastro* and down the beach to the main jetty where a woman stood waiting, her face alight with laughter as she held out her arms.

'Surprise!'

'You certainly are!' He hugged her tightly for a long moment, then held her away from him and raised a mocking eyebrow. 'You were just passing?'

Talia Kazan's eyes sparkled as she smiled up into the hard, handsome face. 'Passing! I've been travelling for so long I hardly know what day it is!'

He motioned to the beaming Yannis to help bring the bags. 'Give it up, Mother, the ditzy-blonde act doesn't work with me. You know exactly what day it is.'

She shrugged, unrepentant. 'Who better? I had a sudden desire to see my son so I packed my bags and came to do that—you are pleased, I trust?'

He kissed the hand he was holding. 'Of course; I'm delighted! But you took a risk. I might not have been here.'

Her eyes gleamed in triumph. 'Since I am *not* ditzy, I contacted your admirable Stefan to make sure you would be here for the festival and swore him to silence. He said you were coming alone, as usual.' She shook her head in reproof. 'You should have brought some pleasant company with you.'

'If by pleasant you mean female, the women I know demand the sophisticated pleasures of the city, Mother. Arcane festivals on a remote island just don't do it for them.'

'Then invite someone with a higher cultural threshold.' The luminous violet eyes were suddenly serious. 'It is time you put that nonsense from Christina Mavros behind you and found a real woman.'

He shrugged that off with an impatient smile. 'Did Takis bring you over?'

'No; he was so busy over there with guests checking in at the *taverna*. A very kind young man assured me it was a pleasure to bring me to Kyrkiros and so save Takis the trouble.'

'Who was this man?' demanded her son sharply.

'I did not catch his name over the noise of the boat engine. Now, lead me to Sofia so I can beg her for coffee.'

Sofia and her crew were clustered at the kitchen door, faces wreathed in smiles as they greeted '*kyria* Talia' in rapture and pressed her to have coffee, wine, pastries or anything her heart desired that they could provide.

One of the new arrivals on the neighbouring island of Karpyros felt a rush of excitement as she focused her discreet little binoculars on the action across the water. At this distance it was hard to be sure, but the man hugging a blonde over there surely had to be the rare sight of Alexei Drakos, the boy-wonder entrepreneur famed for his hostility towards the media.

Eleanor tucked the binoculars away when her lunch arrived and with a smile thanked the young waiter in the basic Greek she'd crammed for her current assignment: a series of travel articles on lesser-known Greek islands well off the tourist trail. It was more ambitious than anything she'd worked on to date, and before grudgingly signing off on expenses her editor had dropped a bombshell by stipulating a shot at an interview with Alexei Drakos as part of the deal.

'Since the Mavros woman did the dirty on him a few months ago, he's kept a very low profile, but apparently he always visits his island in June. Make damn sure you get there in good time because tourists swarm there for some festival he's put on every year since he bought the island. There's no accommodation, so book a room somewhere else, plus a boat to get you there on the day.' Ross McLean had flashed his bleached veneers at her. 'And wear something sexy to beard the lion in his den.'

'Drakos translates as dragon, not lion,' she'd retorted. 'And I don't do sexy!'

On her way out Eleanor had heard him muttering about college girls who thought they knew it all and rolled her eyes. There was fat chance of getting a reporter's job these days without a college degree, and to augment hers she'd worked her socks off to add photography to her journalism qualifications; something greatly to her advantage with Ross McLean because it saved him the expense of a photographer.

Now she was almost literally in sight of her quarry, Eleanor refused to spoil her appetite by worrying about how to achieve the scoop her boss was so hot for. But succeed she would, somehow, if only to show him just what a 'college girl' could do. Maybe the reclusive Mr Drakos would be in a sociable mood now the blonde had arrived to keep him company. Though Ross, drat the man, knew very well he was asking the impossible. Alexei Drakos had been famous for stonewalling journalists even before the lurid exposé by a furious ex-lover. But who had he been hugging today? No matter how hard she'd dug, Eleanor had learned frustratingly little about the man's private life other than the woman-scorned outpourings of Christina Mavros. Her research into his professional persona had built up a picture of a *wunderkind* who achieved success while still at school with some kind of genius software technology, and as an adult entrepreneur went on to put his money to good use with investments in pharmaceuticals, property and more technology.

But, other than his reputation for philanthropy she had no clue to the man behind the public persona.

The taverna owner's son rushed over as Eleanor got up to leave and carried her luggage the short distance to one of the small apartments. He set her bags down on the small veranda fronting the last of the square white cubes overlooking the harbour and unlocked the blue door. Eleanor smiled in approval at the scrupulously clean, white-walled room as Petros carried her bags inside and told him she intended dining at the taverna that night.

'Then I will reserve a table for you, *kyria*. Many people will be here tonight before the festival tomorrow,' he told her, and flushed with pleasure when she thanked him and gave him a hefty tip.

Petros was right, of course. The place would be heaving with visitors ready to swarm across to Kyrkiros tomorrow. But if Alexei Drakos was such a private man why did he open his island to all and sundry, even if it was for just one day? While she dined later she could gaze across the sea and speculate to her heart's content about the king of the Kastro on the island over there. In the meantime, she'd haul her bags up the ladder to

the open mezzanine bedroom, do her usual mini-
mum unpacking and take a short nap.

Eleanor showered later in the tiny, spotless bathroom and dressed in her usual trademark jeans
and T-shirt. As a gesture to the island night-life
the jeans were white and the clinging top black
and scooped low enough to show a hint of sun-
tanned cleavage; and in a practice run for dragon-
slaying the next day, she brushed on mascara and
lip gloss. Eleanor eyed her reflection critically.
Two weeks of island-hopping in the sun had added
a satisfactory bronze glow to her skin, but the effect was more healthy than sexy. She shrugged.
If Ross was rat enough to fire her for failing to
get the exclusive he was panting for, she would
go freelance.

The taverna was buzzing with holidaymakers
and locals when Petros darted out to conduct her
to a tiny table which gave her a good view across
the boats bobbing in the harbour to the lights just
visible on the dark outline of Kyrkiros on the hori-
zon. She was served with bread and olives to nib-
ble on while she waited for the red mullet, which
arrived sizzling, dressed with lemon juice and

olive oil, and accompanied by a salad and half a carafe of local wine.

Eleanor thanked Petros warmly and asked about the festival next day. 'Is the bull dance for men only?'

He shook his head. 'The *taurokathapsia* is for both men and women. Enjoy your meal, *kyria*.'

Eleanor peered at the distant lights across the water, wondering about Alexei Drakos. From what little she'd learned about his personal life, it seemed unlikely he was looking forward to the invasion on his territory next day, but at least he now had the blonde to cheer him up when the hoi polloi descended on him. Her research might have turned up nothing about any current love life, but she'd made the deeply intriguing discovery that his mother had been one of the most famous photographic models of her day. Talia Kazan's heyday had been short. Her exquisite face had never graced magazine covers again after she married Milo Drakos and produced the son who, allegedly, was estranged from his father. Eleanor's journalistic antennae buzzed like bees with the urge to find out why.

As she left the taverna Eleanor complimented

the owner about her dinner, and when she ordered lunch for next day remembered to confirm that a boat had been booked for her trip over to Kyrkiros afterwards. Once there her plan was to soak up the festival atmosphere, take lots of photographs and then sit back people-watching at her reserved table while she waited for the lord and master of the island to show. Or not.

Back in her room, Eleanor soon regretted her nap. After a while she gave up trying to sleep and switched on her laptop to do more digging. She went back to the piece about Christina Mavros, the socialite from Crete who had failed in her aim to marry Alexei Drakos and subsequently sold her vindictive, highly coloured story to the press. Stupid woman, thought Eleanor as she went on with her search, but by the time her eyes began to droop at last her only new find had been a photograph of Alexei's father. From the cut of his hard, handsome face it seemed that Milo Drakos would make a bad enemy.

Eleanor woke late next morning and hurriedly climbed down the ladder to make coffee to kick-start the day. After her shower she followed Ross McLean's instructions and pulled on a dress for once, instead of jeans. Not that it was remotely the kind of thing her boss had in mind. The navy-striped white Breton number was as simple and comfortable as a T-shirt, but at least it showed off legs the Greek sun had toasted to an even darker shade of bronze than her face.

Later on at the taverna, Eleanor enjoyed an entertaining lunch hour as she watched seagoing craft of all descriptions making for the other island. When Petros finally came to say her boat was waiting for her, the sun was so fierce she was glad of dark glasses and sun hat for the trip across the sea, her excitement mounting at the approach to the steep, rocky island dominated by an ancient kastro. She breathed in the familiar sage and lavender scent of the Greek *maquis* lining the paths winding up through sun-baked hillside; the sound of music and chattering crowds in festive mood added to her anticipation as her genial ferryman docked at a jetty.

Eleanor thanked him and settled a time for the trip back later that evening, then got straight to work to take shots of the houses which clustered around the Kastro and climbed the slopes above it to a summit crowned by the blue dome of an icing-white church. Groundwork done, she threaded her way through the chattering, animated crowds to claim the place she'd reserved at one of the tables under the pergola. Musicians were playing at the far end of the terrace, but she'd learned from Petros that the main event would be after dark when bonfires were lit for the performance of the famous bull dance. She eyed the stage with misgiving. She'd seen pictures of the frescoes on Crete, depicting dancers somersaulting over a bull, but there was no visible way to restrain an animal here if it got out of hand, which was worrying.

She promptly forgot about bulls when the doors to the Kastro opened and three people emerged to descend the steps to the terrace. Of the two men in the group, it was obvious who was king of this particular castle. Alexei Drakos was smiling down at his blonde companion, and Eleanor realised in sudden excitement that she was Talia Kazan in the flesh, from this distance as beautiful in maturity as she had been in her heyday. The blonde was no pillow-friend after all, but Alexei's mother, in a hyacinth-blue dress of exquisite cut, a large straw hat on her gleaming hair.

The son was equally striking. His curling hair

was only a few shades darker gold than his mother's, instead of black as Eleanor had expected before she'd researched him, but his face was carved from different, utterly masculine clay, with heavy-lidded dark eyes and handsome, forceful features which bore an unmistakeable resemblance to his father. He was slim-hipped and broad shouldered, and even in conventional linen trousers and white shirt, which merely hinted at the muscles beneath, there was a powerful masculine grace about him. Alexei Drakos was a magnificent specimen of manhood by any standards.

Eleanor watched, riveted, as Alexei linked his arm through his mother's to inspect the goods on display at each stall for a brief moment and exchange a few words with the vendors before leaving the field clear to the purchasing public. From under cover of her table's parasol, Eleanor took a few shots of mother and son with the Kastro as backdrop then turned her lens on the festive crowd milling about in the hot sunshine.

Eventually she put her camera away and went off to browse among the stalls for presents to take home. The crafts on display were of good quality. She soon found carved worry-beads that would

amuse her father and a small, exquisitely embroi-
dered picture perfect for her mother. With regret
she passed by the displays of pottery and copper
pots as too difficult to transport home, but then
reached a stall with goods that made her mouth
water. She'd read that it was hard to find really
good jewellery outside the larger towns in Greece,
but the wares on sale here were the real deal and
obviously came from the mainland. When enough
space cleared to let her get a look, she passed
over the striking pendants and earrings way out
of her price range and concentrated on trays of
small trinkets, one of which caught her eye and
said 'buy me'.

'Copy of Minoan ornament,' the man on the
stall stated, but in such strongly accented Greek
Eleanor barely understood. 'You like it?'

The tiny crystal bull had a gold loop on its back;
perfect to attach to her charm bracelet. She liked
it a lot.

'How much?' she asked, but when he mentioned
the sum she shook her head regretfully, which
prompted an unintelligible spiel from him on the
virtues of the charm. The man only broke off
when space was made for someone who addressed

Eleanor in Greek to ask if she needed help with the problem. Her most immediate problem, due to the sudden sight and scent of Alexei Drakos at such close quarters, was trying to muster enough breath and vocabulary to answer.

'I don't speak enough Greek to bargain,' she said at last in English.

'Ah, I see. Allow me.' He began a rapid exchange with the stall holder and turned to Eleanor with a smile that rocked her on her heels as he named a price just within her budget.

'Thank you so much!' She hastily counted out money to hand over before the stall holder could change his mind, and tried to concentrate as the man said a lot more she couldn't understand. Standing so close to Alexei Drakos was scrambling her brain!

'He will attach it to your bracelet if you leave it with him for a while,' he translated for her, the hint of attractive accent adding to her problem.

'Thank you.' Eleanor unfastened the heavy gold chain from her wrist and handed it to the vendor, pointing to a link near the lock.

'I told him to bring it to you later,' said Alexei. 'Do you have a table?'

Eleanor nodded dumbly, certain by now he thought she was a total idiot.

'Alexei *mou*, I heard you speaking English,' said his mother, hurrying to join them. 'Won't you introduce me?'

He smiled. 'I've only just met the lady myself.'

'Then I will make the introductions. I am Talia Kazan, and this is my son, Alexei Drakos.' Her accent was equally fascinating, but more pronounced than her son's, the words spoken with friendly warmth that unlocked Eleanor's tongue.

'Eleanor Markham,' she said, smiling. 'How do you do?'

'Delighted to meet you. Are you here with friends?'

'No, I'm travelling alone.'

'Then would you care to join me for a drink?' said Talia.

Would she! Eleanor beamed. 'I'd love to. Perhaps you'd come over to my table.'

'I'll send someone,' said Alexei, and went off to speak to a waiter.

Talia gave Eleanor the smile that had made her famous. 'I am so glad of some company. Alex is very busy today.' When they reached the table, to the intense interest of people sitting nearby, she sat down with a sigh of pleasure. 'Are you just here for the day at the festival, or are you staying on Karpyros?'

Eleanor explained about her assignment.

Talia's violet eyes were instantly guarded. 'You are a journalist.'

Eleanor met the look steadily. 'Yes. But I'm not a gossip columnist. I work in features, mainly on travel, so I won't capitalise on meeting the famous Talia Kazan.'

The slender shoulders shrugged. 'It is a very long time since I was famous.'

'Yet you've hardly changed at all.' Eleanor spoke with such obvious sincerity the beautiful eyes warmed.

'How kind of you to say so. You are here to write about the festival?'

Eleanor nodded, hoping she didn't look guilty. Bad move to reveal that an interview with Alexei Drakos was her main objective.

'I have not been here for the festival for a while,' Talia told her. 'But Alex always leaves his calendar clear for it, so I came on impulse to surprise him.'

'He must have been delighted!'

'Fortunately, he seemed to be. Not every man welcomes a surprise visit from his mother.' Talia smiled up at the youth setting down glasses, bottles of mineral water and fruit juice. *'Efcharisto,* Yannis.' She eyed Eleanor with gratifying interest. 'So, tell me about your assignment.'

Eleanor described the lesser-known islands she'd visited for her series. 'I take my own photographs, so I nearly always travel solo.'

'But you must have someone in the UK waiting impatiently for your return?' The blue eyes sparkled, unashamedly curious.

Eleanor shook her head, smiling. 'The only one waiting impatiently right now is my editor. But I'm lucky enough to have good friends, and I'm close to my parents.'

'I am most fortunate myself that way. My son may be a busy man, but he makes time for regular—if brief—visits to his mother. Do you live at home with your parents?'

Before Eleanor could reply, Alexei Drakos joined them.

Talia smiled at him warmly. 'Sit with us for a while.'

He shook his head. 'Stefan tells me I have calls to return. Miss Markham, has your bracelet been returned to you?'

'No, not yet.'

'I'll hurry the man along.' With an abstracted smile, he strode off again.

His mother looked after him anxiously. 'The world does not leave him alone, even here at his retreat—though Stefan, his assistant, does his best to keep it at bay over this particular holiday.'

'This festival is obviously important to—to your son,' said Eleanor.

'To me, also,' said Talia, and looked up with an enquiring smile as a boy approached the table, holding out a package.

'Ah, that must be for me,' said Eleanor, and took out her bracelet, now adorned with the crystal bull. '*Efcharisto*!' she said, pleased, and handed over a tip. She smiled guiltily as she displayed the charm. 'Very expensive, but I couldn't resist it after your son was kind enough to bargain the price down.'

Talia leaned closer to examine it. 'Exquisite— and a most perfect souvenir of Kyrkiros.'

Eleanor fastened the bracelet on her wrist. 'There. No more extravagance for me this trip.'

Alexei Drakos' assistant came towards them, smiling respectfully. 'Forgive me for interrupting, but Sofia says a light supper is ready, *kyria* Talia. She apologises it is early tonight because of the *taurokathapsia*.'

'Of course,' she said, getting up. 'Miss Eleanor Markham, meet Stefan Petrides, Alexei's man in Athens.'

Stefan bowed formally to Eleanor. '*Chairo poly, kyria* Markham.'

'*Pos eiste*,' she returned.

'I am not happy leaving you alone here, my dear,' said Talia, frowning. 'Please join us for dinner.'

Eleanor smiled gratefully, but shook her head. 'That's so kind of you, but I purposely ate enough lunch to see me through the evening. Goodbye— it's been such a pleasure to meet you.'

'Likewise, Eleanor Markham, though the day is not over yet,' said Talia, and with a smile went off with her escort.

Eleanor gazed after them a little wistfully, then sat down and began writing up the events of the afternoon. She was soon so deeply absorbed she jumped when someone rapped on the metal table. She looked up with a smile to find Alexei Drakos eyeing her notebook with hostility.

'My mother is concerned about leaving you alone here,' he said coldly. 'But you're obviously busy. She tells me you're a journalist.'

Her smile died. 'Yes, I am.'

'And my island is providing an even richer source of material than you expected?'

Eleanor's defences sprang to attention. 'It is indeed.'

'Write one word about my mother, and I will sue,' he said with menace.

Eleanor's chin went up. 'I'm here solely to report on this famous festival of yours, Mr Drakos. But, since you ask so *nicely,* I'll leave out my chance meeting with Talia Kazan. Though, since I would be reporting fact, suing would not be possible.'

'Maybe not.' His cold eyes locked on hers. 'But believe me, Miss Markham—whatever rag you work for I can get you fired as easily as I helped you out earlier.'

He strode off, cursing at the chance that had involved his mother with Eleanor Markham. Since the notoriety Christina Mavros had brought on him, he had avoided contact with any woman other than his mother. Until today, that was, when an attractive tourist's rueful little smile had seduced him into offering help to someone who was not only a woman but a reporter, for God's sake!

Eleanor stared after him balefully. No chance of an interview with Talia Kazan's baby boy, then. And no prize for guessing how Alexei Drakos had made his fortune, either. He'd probably just stepped on the necks of everyone who got in his way. Her mouth tightened. Romantic fool that she was, the chance meeting with him had been one of the major experiences of her life, whereas to him she was just a petty little problem to solve by threats.

Her eyes sparking like an angry cat's behind her glasses, she noted that all the reserved tables were now full, other than the one adjoining hers. Everyone was eating and drinking and having a wonderful time in laughing, animated groups, which emphasized her solitary state—a common enough situation on her travels, and not one that had bothered her in the slightest up to now. Eleanor shrugged impatiently. Her blood sugars obviously needed a boost after the clash with the dragon of Kyrkiros. She walked over to the stalls, bought a couple of nut-filled honey pastries from one of them, and returned to her table to find a teenaged lad waiting there.

'*Kyria* Talia sent for you,' he informed her, indicating the tray on the table.

Eleanor smiled warmly and asked him to convey her thanks to the lady. She sat down to pour tea into a delicate china cup and smiled when she tasted an unmistakeably British blend. The pastries were doubly delicious with the tea as accompaniment. By the time Eleanor had finished her surprise treat, lamps were glowing along the terrace, the sudden darkness of the Aegean night had fallen, a singer had joined the musicians and she had almost recovered from the blow of her encounter with Alexei Drakos. She stiffened when an audible ripple of interest through the crowd heralded the arrival of the man himself as he ushered his mother to the adjoining table. One look at him revived her anger so fiercely it took an effort to smile when Talia beckoned to her.

'Do come and join us, Eleanor. The dancing will start soon.'

Eleanor shook her head firmly; grateful it was too dark for her feelings to show. 'It's very kind of you but I wouldn't dream of intruding.'

'Nonsense! Why sit there alone? Stefan will bring your things.'

And, short of causing a scene, Eleanor was obliged to accept the chair Alexei Drakos held out for her next to his mother. She thanked him politely and smiled at Talia. 'And thank *you* so much for the tea. It was just what I needed.'

'I hoped it might be. I made it with my own fair hands.' The radiance of Talia's smile contrasted sharply with the expression on her son's face. 'Do stop looming over us and sit down, Alexei *mou*— you too, Stefan.'

Eleanor tensed, her stomach muscles contracting as a bull bellowed somewhere deep inside the *Kastro*, loud enough to be heard above the music and the noise of the chattering crowd.

'Ah, we begin,' said Talia with satisfaction.

Alexei eyed Eleanor sardonically. 'Is something wrong, Miss Markham?'

'Nothing at all,' she lied, but sucked in a startled breath as the lights died. They were left in darkness for several tense seconds before the torches encircling the raised wooden platform burst into flame, and bonfires ignited one after the other along the outer edges of the beach.

'How is that for Greek drama?' crowed Talia, touching Eleanor's hand. 'My dear, you are so cold. What is wrong?'

'Anticipation,' Eleanor said brightly. With a defiant look at Alexei Drakos, she took out her camera. 'For my article,' she informed him.

'You may take as many photographs of the dancers as you wish,' he assured her, his message loud and clear. One shot of his beautiful mother and Eleanor Markham would be thrown off his island.

'Thank you.' She turned her attention to the stage, intrigued to see that the musicians had exchanged their modern instruments for harps and flutes which looked like museum exhibits. Along with some kind of snare drums, they began to make music so eerily unlike anything she'd ever heard before the hairs rose on the back of her neck and her blood began to pulse in time with the hypnotic beat.

With sudden drama, the great *Kastro* doors were flung open and a roar of applause greeted the dancers who came out two by two, moving in a slow rhythm dictated by the drum beat as they descended to the terrace. At first sight Eleanor thought they were all men after all, but when they moved into the dramatic ring of torchlight the girls among them were obvious by the bandeaux covering their breasts. Otherwise all the dancers wore loin guards under brief, gauzy kilts, glinting gold jewellery, black wigs with ringlets and soft leather sandals laced high up the leg.

Eleanor forgot Alexei Drakos' hostility and sat entranced. The entire scene was straight off a painting on some ancient vase, except that these figures were alive and moving. The procession circled the torch-lit stage twice in hypnotic, slow-stepping rhythm before the dancers lined up in a double row to look up at the table where Alexei Drakos sat with his guests. The leader, a muscular figure with eyes painted as heavily as the girls, stepped forward to salute Alexei and Eleanor shook herself out of her trance to capture the scene on film in the instant before the lithe figures began to dance. They swayed in perfect unison, dipping and weaving in sinuous, labyrinthine patterns which gradually grew more and more complex as the beat of the music quickened. It rose faster and faster to a final crescendo as a bull bellowed off-stage, the doors burst open again and a figure out of myth and nightmare gave a great leap down into the torchlight. The crowd went wild at the sight of a black bull's head with crystal eyes and vicious horns topping a muscular, human male body.

CHAPTER TWO

ELEANOR'S relief was so intense she had to wait until her hands were steady enough to do the job she'd come for as she focused her lens on the fantastic figure. She smiled in recognition as a new player leapt into the torchlight to face the beast, the testosterone in every line of the bronzed muscular body in sharp contrast to his painted face and golden love-locks; Theseus, the blond Hellene, come to slay the Minotaur.

Eleanor took several shots then sat, mesmerised, as Theseus and the dancers swooped around the central half-man half-beast figure, taunting him like a flock of mockingbirds as they somersaulted away from his lunging horns. She gasped with the audience as Theseus vaulted from the bent back of one of the male dancers to somersault through the air over the Minotaur's horns. He landed on his feet with the grace and skill of an Olympic gymnast, an imperious hand raised to hush the applause as the troupe launched into a series of athletic, balance-defying somersaults, spinning around the central figure while the Minotaur lunged at them in graphically conveyed fury. In perfect rhythm the dancers taunted him with their dizzying kaleidoscope of movement as again and again Theseus danced away from the menacing horns. The music grew more and more frenzied until the dance culminated in another breath-taking somersault by Theseus over the great bull's head, but this time he snatched up a golden double-headed axe of the type Eleanor had seen in photographs of Cretan artefacts.

The Minotaur lunged with such ferocity the audience gave a great, concerted gasp again as Theseus leapt aside to avoid the horns and held the axe aloft for an instant of pure drama, before bringing it down on the Minotaur's neck. There was an anguished bellow as the man-beast sank slowly to his knees and then fell, sprawled, the great horned head at Theseus's feet.

To say the crowd went wild again was an understatement. But, even as Eleanor applauded with the rest, her inner cynic warned that the sheer drama of the moment would end when the beast was obliged to get to his all-too-human feet as the performers took their bow. But, though the applause was prolonged, there was no bow. Still blank-faced as figures on a fresco, the dancers formed a line on either side of the fallen figure. With Theseus and the lead dancer at the impressive shoulders, the male members of the troupe bent as one man to pick up the Minotaur and heaved him up in a practised movement to shoulder height. The women went ahead, hands clasped and heads bowed as, still in rhythm with the wailing flutes and now slow, solemn, hypnotic drumbeat, the vanquished man-beast was slowly borne around the torch-lit arena, horned head hanging, then up the steep steps and through the double doors into the Kastro, to tumultuous applause and cheers from the crowd.

'So what did you think of our famous *taurokathapsia*, Ms Markham?' asked Alexei Drakos as the musicians took up their modern instruments again. 'You seemed nervous before it started. Were you expecting something different?'

'Yes.' She exchanged a rueful smile with Talia. 'I was afraid a real live bull was involved.'

'I rather fancied you were, but I couldn't spoil

the drama by reassuring you!' Talia smiled indulgently and exchanged a glance with her son. 'Was the dance originally done with an actual animal?'

'According to myth and legend, yes, and the wall paintings on Knossos in Crete seem to bear that out. But not here.' He looked very deliberately at Eleanor. 'I assure you that no bulls have danced on Kyrkiros since I acquired the island. Though I can't answer for what happened back in prehistory, Ms Markham.' He beckoned to Yannis, who came hurrying to ask what the *'kyrie'* desired, and Alexei turned to Stefan.

'Join your friends now, if you like. I shan't need you anymore tonight,' he said in English.

'Thank you, *kyrie*,' the young man replied. '*Kalinychta*, ladies. This has been a great pleasure.'

'Thank you for your company, Stefan.' Talia gave him her hand. He kissed it formally, bowed to Eleanor and hurried off to the far end of the terrace, where he was absorbed into an exuberant crowd at one of the tables.

'So, what would you like?' asked Alexei.

Talia asked for coffee. 'After all the emotion

expended on that performance, I am not hungry. How about you, Eleanor?'

'Coffee would be wonderful, thank you.' Eleanor glanced at her watch as Yannis hurried off with the order. 'I'll be leaving soon.'

'How are you getting back?' asked Talia.

'The boatman who brought me is coming to pick me up.' Eleanor smiled at her gratefully. 'Thank you so much for inviting me to join you.'

'We were very pleased to have your company.' Talia fixed her son with an imperious blue gaze. 'Were we not, Alex?'

'Delighted.' He looked directly at Eleanor. 'Do you have all you require for your article?'

She nodded. 'Your festival will make a wonderful finale to my series. Of course, I'll make it clear that this is an annual event, and stress that Kyrkiros is a private island, not a holiday destination. Was the original bull dance performed as a mid-summer celebration?'

'According to historians it was probably a regular attraction on Crete.'

'It is performed here at this time to commemorate the feast of St John, which also happens to be Alex's birthday,' said Talia, with a smile for her son.

'Then I wish you many happy returns, Mr Drakos,' Eleanor said with formality. 'As I said earlier, nothing will appear in my article that you could object to.'

'Earlier?' said Talia sharply.

Her son shrugged. 'I had a conversation with Ms Markham on the subject of reprisals. I told her what would happen if she mentioned your name.'

His mother stared at him, appalled. 'You *threatened* her?'

'Yes,' he said, unmoved. 'She may write all she wants about the festival and the island. But if there's a single reference to you personally, I'll sue the paper she works for.'

Crimson to the roots of her hair, Eleanor stared at her watch, willing the hands to move faster as Talia shook her head in disbelief.

'Forgive my son, Eleanor. He is absurdly protective about me.' She frowned at him. 'After all, even if I was mentioned, who would remember me after all these years?'

'Don't be naive, Mother.' His mouth tightened

when Talia very deliberately poured only two cups of coffee.

'We shall excuse you now, Alexei,' she informed him sweetly. 'You must have people to see.'

Eleanor thoroughly enjoyed the sight of Alexei Drakos dismissed with such relentless grace.

He got to his feet, and gave Eleanor a cool nod. 'I'll say goodbye then, Miss Markham.'

She inclined her head in cool response. 'Goodbye.'

'I'll come back for you after your guest leaves,' he informed his mother.

She smiled indulgently. 'I am perfectly capable of walking indoors on my own, Alexei.'

'I will come back for you,' he said with finality.

Talia sighed as she watched him go. 'My dear, I promise you that Alex will not carry out his threat.'

'It won't be necessary. I won't say a word about you in my article—hugely tempting though it would be,' admitted Eleanor. 'But I confess that I've taken a couple of photographs of you, Ms Kazan—purely personal shots to show my mother. She was a huge fan of yours.'

Talia smiled radiantly. 'Really? I fear she will

be disappointed to see me as I am now. I would not have been brave enough for cosmetic surgery—not that I had the slightest need to bother, once I left the cameras behind. These days I use so-called miracle creams and try not to eat too many wicked things—like Sofia's savoury pastries, which are my guilty pleasure. I should have ordered some for you to try, Eleanor.'

'I'm sure they're delicious, but I'm not hungry.'

Talia frowned. 'My son upset you so much?'

Eleanor shrugged, smiling. 'A thick skin is a basic requirement in my profession.'

Talia Kazan was so easy to talk to, Eleanor had soon described previous assignments and felt guilty when Yannis came to inform them a man was asking for the *kyria* at the ferry. 'I've been talking so much I forgot the time!'

'And I have enjoyed listening!' Talia told Yannis he could go, that she would accompany her guest to the boat herself.

'Your son won't like that,' said Eleanor quickly, and cast a glance along the terrace, where Alexei Drakos was talking to the troupe of dancers, who looked very different out of costume.

'My dear, Alex can play the autocrat as much

as he likes with the rest of the world, but not with me.' Talia's smile cleared a way for them through the crowd. 'Yannis said the south jetty, which is odd, because it's so much farther away. No matter; a little exercise is good, yes?'

Eleanor disagreed, growing more and more uneasy when she found that the jetty in question was on one of the beaches out of bounds to the public, with no bonfires to guide them. Her misgiving intensified once they'd moved out of range of the Kastro lights. It was hard to make out the path to the jetty and progress was slow.

'Follow me,' said Talia. 'I know the way. Keep close behind—' She gave a sudden shriek as a dark figure shot out of the shadows and snatched her up in his arms to make a run for the jetty. In knee-jerk reaction, Eleanor tore after him as Talia screamed for her son and struggled so fiercely the man stumbled, cursing, and dropped his flailing burden. Eleanor swung her tote bag at his head while he was still staggering and sent him down hard on the jetty, then jumped on him and got in a few punches before he reared up with a furious roar and kicked her into the sea. She sank like a stone and panicked for endless moments until self-preservation instincts finally kicked in. Lungs bursting, she managed to swim up to the surface, coughing and spluttering, and struggling wildly against powerful arms that restrained her.

'Stop!' panted Alexei Drakos. 'I'm trying to rescue you, woman.'

Limp with relief, Eleanor let him tow her through the water to thrust her up into Stefan's grasp before heaving himself out of the water onto the jetty.

'Is your mother safe?' Eleanor demanded hoarsely, and then wrenched herself away from Stefan to cough up more of the Aegean as Talia pushed him aside to get to her.

'Tell me exactly what happened, Mother!' ordered Alexei, thrusting wet hair back from his face.

While Eleanor coughed up more water, Talia explained breathlessly up to the point where the attacker dropped her. 'Then this brave, brave girl knocked him down with her bag and beat him up.'

'But not hard enough. The swine kicked me into the water,' croaked Eleanor hoarsely through chattering teeth. 'Did he get away?'

Alexei's smile turned her blood even colder. 'No, he did not.'

'Where is he?'

'On his way to the Kastro, in company with a pair of angry jailers.'

'Excellent! We should go inside, too,' said Talia firmly. 'You two need to get dry.'

Alexei turned as Yannis came hurrying to say that someone else was asking for the *kyria*. 'What the devil now?' he demanded irritably, turning on Eleanor.

'It must be the real boatman—the one who brought me here earlier,' she said through chattering teeth.

'So, how did the other man contact you?'

'Yannis told us a man was waiting at the jetty,' explained Talia.

Alexei spoke to the boy sharply and, after listening to his explanation, gave him instructions which sent him running off into the Kastro to fetch his mother. 'Apparently our prisoner said he was here for the lady. Yannis knew you were about to leave, Miss Markham, so assumed it was you.'

'Then I'm to blame. I'm so *sorry*,' croaked Eleanor in remorse, but Talia shook her head fiercely.

'Nonsense, it was not your fault!'

By this time Eleanor was so desperate to get back to the taverna and a hot shower she was past caring whose fault it was. 'Now my real ferryman has arrived, I'll take myself off—'

'Absolutely not, Eleanor,' Talia said flatly, and beckoned to the woman hurrying towards them with towels. 'This is Sofia, the housekeeper here. I'll explain to her and then we'll soon have you in a hot bath and into bed.'

'But I can't do that! I need to pay the boatman and get back to the taverna,' protested Eleanor hoarsely, turning away to cough.

'Stefan will see to that—also, send a message to Takis,' said Alexei. 'You must stay here until I interrogate the kidnapper. In the meantime, go indoors with my mother—please,' he added.

'My bag!' said Eleanor in sudden alarm.

'The assault weapon?' His lips twitched as he handed it over. 'Stefan rescued it, but I can't answer for the contents.'

'I hope your camera is undamaged!' exclaimed Talia.

'If not, I shall replace it,' said Alexei, shrugging.

'That won't be necessary, thank you.' Eleanor breathed more easily as she investigated. 'My phone took a direct hit, and the glass on a picture I bought for my mother is cracked. But the camera seems all right.' She was horribly conscious of her bedraggled appearance as Talia bundled her up in a towel. So much for looking sexy! 'The memory card will have survived, anyway. I won't lose any of the pictures.'

'Excellent. Now we must go inside and get something hot into both of you.' Talia spoke to Sofia, who nodded vigorously and hurried off.

To Eleanor's surprise the musicians were still playing and singing on the terrace, people were talking at the tops of their voices at the tables and a large crowd was still milling around on the beach, where youngsters were shouting as they took turns in leaping over the traditional St John's bonfires. 'Didn't they hear all the commotion?'

'Too much noise, and I got there so quickly I doubt that anyone noticed,' said Alexei, rubbing his hair. 'I followed when I saw you leave the table with my mother and hurried after you in time to hear her scream for me. But I regret that I arrived too late to stop the intruder kicking you into the water. Stefan and a couple of my security men were behind me as I caught him, and they took charge of him while I went in after you.'

'I wish I'd known all that when I was trying not to drown,' said Eleanor wryly.

'Alex dived in after you almost at once,' Talia assured her.

My hero, thought Eleanor, and won herself a sharp look from her dripping rescuer as he escorted them into the cavernous hall of the Kastro and into the anachronism of a modern lift. After a swift, quiet ascent it opened onto the hall of an apartment that could have been part of a modern building. Impressed by the contrast to the ancient Kastro which housed it, Eleanor wrapped her towels around her more tightly to avoid wetting the beautiful floor as Talia led her to a surprisingly feminine bedroom.

'You must get into my shower, as hot as you can bear it. You've lost your lovely glow.'

'You look pale yourself,' said Eleanor anxiously. 'You had a horrible shock, too.'

'But I wasn't kicked into the sea, my dear! Use any of my bath stuff you want.'

'Thank you.' Eleanor's teeth began chattering again.

Talia wagged a finger. 'Be quick; you need something hot to drink. Wrap yourself in the bathrobe behind the door.'

Eleanor bundled her sodden clothes up in the damp towel and put them in the slipper-shaped bath. To her relief her waterproof watch had survived undamaged and, even more miraculously, the crystal bull-charm was still intact on her chain bracelet. Feeling limp as a rag doll as her adrenaline drained away, she turned on hot water in the shower and used some of Talia's shampoo. After a few warming minutes under the spray to rinse her hair she dried off, wincing as she encountered various aches and pains, the most painful a large welt on her ribcage, courtesy of a male shoe. Swathed in towels, she slumped down suddenly on the edge of the elegant bath. What a day! She brightened suddenly as she rubbed at her hair. Now she'd helped save his mother from kidnap, maybe Alexei Drakos would give her an interview by way of thanks. And maybe the moon would turn blue tonight!

Eleanor ran one of his combs through her hair,

eyed her reflection without pleasure and reached for the hooded white bathrobe on the door. She replaced her watch and bracelet and opened the door in answer to a quiet knock.

Talia came in, wrapped in a long navy bathrobe, her wet hair tied back from her beautiful face. 'You feel better now, Eleanor?' she asked anxiously as she applied moisturiser.

'Lots better, thank you. How about you?'

Talia grimaced. 'I stripped off every stitch after contact with that man. I had a quick shower in Alex's bathroom and borrowed his bathrobe so, now I have washed away *eau de kidnapper,* I am fine.'

'Thank God for that,' said Eleanor fervently. 'What shall I do with my wet clothes?'

'Sofia will deal with them. She has brought food to the tower room, so come and eat something.'

Suddenly so tired she wanted nothing more than to crawl into the nearest bed and sleep, Eleanor followed Talia to a room with a panoramic sweep of windows and a tray with savoury steam rising from it on a low table in front of a huge leather sofa.

'Sofia's special lentil soup will get you warm,'

said Talia. 'After all this drama, you need something nourishing.' She shuddered. 'I thought I was done for when that monster grabbed me, but you attacked him like an avenging fury.'

'He made me so angry,' agreed Eleanor, and took the bowl Talia handed to her. 'Something exploded inside me when the brute snatched you.' She managed a smile. 'But you were pretty ferocious yourself. Between the two of us, the man must have wondered what hit him.'

'I wrenched my shoe off in the struggle and stabbed at his face with the stiletto heel.' Talia laughed unsteadily. 'What an adventure!' She turned as Alexei, now in dry clothes, came into the room with Stefan. 'Did he tell you anything?'

'Nothing useful,' Alex thrust his fingers through damp curls. 'He was insane with fear, certain I intended to kill him for hurting my mother. But eventually he confessed that he was paid to seize the *kyria* and take her to the man waiting at the jetty in a boat. The "dog" who left him to my mercy without paying him.'

'And just who *was* the man in the boat?'

'A stranger he met on Karpyros today who offered him money to do a job for him, if he can be believed. He swears he doesn't know any names, but after some persuasion he gave me his.' Alexei's look chilled Eleanor to the bone. 'He calls himself Spiro Baris, and he's now locked away for the night, moaning about injuries suffered during the struggle.' He shook his head in contempt. 'A struggle with two unarmed women!'

'Not unarmed, exactly. I had my shoe and Eleanor her useful bag,' his mother reminded him, eyes sparkling.

Stefan gave a smothered laugh, and Alexei thawed enough to grin.

'Which of you amazons gave him the black eye?'

'That would probably be me,' said Eleanor, contemplating grazed knuckles. 'I might have got him in the mouth too.'

'You did, *kyria*. He has a split lip,' Stefan said with relish.

'Do you have any other injuries, Eleanor?' asked Alexei.

He'd finally brought himself to use her name! She shook her head. 'A few bruises—the worst one in the ribs from where he kicked me off the jetty.'

'Oh my dear,' said Talia, appalled. 'You must be so sorry you ever set foot on Kyrkiros.'

Alex shot a hard look at Eleanor. 'Will you mention the incident in your article?'

Oh, for heaven's sake! She sucked in a calming breath and winced as her ribs protested. 'And broadcast your breach of security? Of course I won't.'

'Thank you.' He exchanged a glance with Stefan. 'Go down and have a word with Theo. His crew must make very sure no one's stayed behind after the last boat leaves the island.'

'Two of them are guarding the intruder, so I will help him with that,' Stefan said quickly. He wished them goodnight and hurried from the room.

'I'd better get down there too,' said Alexei. He eyed Eleanor with the air of a man with an irritating problem to solve. 'Tomorrow I'm taking my mother to Crete for her return flight to London. You must go with us—Eleanor. I'll try to get you on the same flight.'

'That's very kind of you, but I'm not due back to work for another week.' She smiled politely. 'I've paid out of my own pocket for a week's stay on Karpyros just to lie in the sun and do nothing now I've completed my assignment…' She trailed away at the frowns on both faces.

'It is not wise to do that, dear,' said Talia hastily, before her son could start laying down the law. 'You might get snatched off the beach there.'

Eleanor stared. 'Why? It wasn't me the kidnapper wanted.'

'We can't force you to leave, of course,' said Alexei curtly. 'Think about it while I go down to check with Theo.' He gave his mother a significant look. 'Persuade her, please.'

He strode off to the lift, leaving a tense silence behind him.

'Alex is just trying to do what's best for you,' said Talia soothingly. 'He feels responsible for what happened tonight and wants to keep you safe until you go home. If you go back to Karpyros, he can't do that.'

Eleanor frowned. 'But I'm not his responsibility. It's only natural he's anxious about you, but I'm a complete stranger.'

'Who was injured and half-drowned trying to save his mother from heaven knows what fate. Now show me this bruise.'

Eleanor drew the robe aside from her ribs.

Talia breathed in sharply. 'My dear girl—are you sure nothing is broken in there?'

'Quite sure. I cracked a rib playing hockey in school once, so I know what that feels like. This hurts a bit, but I'll mend.' Eleanor yawned suddenly. 'My wrestling match has left me a bit tired, though. You must be, too. And you must surely have a few bruises yourself!'

Talia nodded ruefully. 'But none as spectacular as yours; the only medication I need is hot tea. I keep a tray in my bedroom, so drink some with me after I see to your hand. I need a talk with Alex before I can think of sleeping.'

'What will he do with the intruder?'

'Call the police here tomorrow to deal with him, I imagine.'

There was something infinitely soothing after all the drama to sit in a comfortable blue velvet chair in Talia's white-painted bedroom, drinking tea from a fine china cup.

'You are quite a girl, Eleanor Markham.' Talia laughed at Eleanor's startled look. 'I mean it. You were very brave tonight.'

'It was pure gut instinct rather than bravery.' Eleanor's eyes flashed angrily. 'I was so furious with the man I wanted to kill him, but in the end the wretch tried to drown me instead.'

'I was in despair until Alex brought you to the surface,' said Talia with a shudder. 'My son was most impressed with you.'

'Only because I attacked the man who tried to kidnap his mother,' Eleanor said flatly. 'This afternoon he was rather less pleasant when he threatened to sue the paper I work for.'

Talia sighed. 'Try to forgive him for that. He is over-protective where I'm concerned. His hostility to the press began when he looked me up online on the computer his father gave him. My ex-husband is a powerful man, but even he failed to stop the speculation about our divorce. Unfortunately, that is the part Alex remembers.' Talia sighed and fixed Eleanor with her famous violet eyes. 'Since then he has further cause to hate the press. You must have researched us before you came. What did you discover?'

'Not that much, except that an ex-girlfriend of your son's sold a colourful story about him to a gossip-column reporter.'

Talia's eyes lit with a tigerish gleam. 'Christina Mavros is a liar, also a fool. She swore she would blacken Alexei's name if he didn't marry her, so he followed your famous Wellington's example and told her to publish and be damned.' She hesitated. 'Did you learn anything about me?'

Eleanor nodded. 'I read that you divorced Milo Drakos—"before the ink was dry on your marriage license", to quote a popular tabloid of the time.'

Talia wrinkled her nose. 'A little exaggerated, but not far out. You must surely want to know why?'

'Of course I do. I'm only human, Ms Kazan.'

'Please—I am Talia!'

Eleanor smiled ruefully. 'I'm wary of appearing familiar. But, just so there's no misunderstanding, none of this will appear in my article. You have my word on it.'

Talia smiled. 'I know that. And I must talk to you about this tonight because Alex is going to rush me away tomorrow and I will not have another chance.'

'For what, exactly?'

'To make a suggestion. If you do not wish to go home yet, why not stay on Kyrkiros until your flight? You will be safe here.'

Eleanor went cold at the mere thought. 'I couldn't possibly.'

'Why not? Once Alex has seen me off at the airport, he can get the ferry back here. I shall insist that he takes a holiday.'

'Even if he agrees, he won't want me around.'

'My son needs to relax, Eleanor, and also needs some intelligent feminine company to relax with. He would never admit it, but his constant aim in life is to achieve bigger and better things than his father.' Talia smiled sadly. 'If you did some research on Milo Drakos, you know that is not easy. It worries me that my son leaves no room in his life for normal relationships. With his looks and money, there have always been women available to him as playmates, but since the affair with Christina Mavros he is wary.' She sighed. 'I so much want him to enjoy the companionship of an intelligent woman. What can I do to persuade you to stay here for a few days and provide him with that?'

Eleanor's first instinct was to assure Talia nothing would persuade her, short of locking her in the Kastro dungeons. But then she had a better idea. 'If you get me an exclusive interview with your son, I will stay for a day or so. My boss is so desperate for his scoop he even ordered me to wear something sexy to persuade your son to talk to me.'

'So you were not really here for the festival at all!'

'Oh yes, *I* was, to round off my series. But Ross McLean is panting for an in-depth interview with the entrepreneur who never talks to reporters. Your son's warning killed all hope of that.' Eleanor looked Talia in the eye. 'But I swear that securing a scoop wasn't my motive for beating off the kidnapper. I just couldn't bear the thought of the man laying hands on someone like you.'

'Someone like me?'

Someone so charming and delicate that the thought of some bruiser manhandling her had sent Eleanor into battle without a second thought. 'Someone I liked so much,' she said, flushing again.

'The feeling is mutual, Eleanor, as I have already made clear.' Talia winced at the sound of raised voices outside. 'What now?'

Alex appeared in the doorway, his face like thunder. 'I apologise for disturbing you, Mother, but we have another intruder. He insists on speaking with you before he leaves.' He turned to the man behind him. 'In deference to our guest, please speak English.'

Talia's eyes widened as Milo Drakos, a commanding figure in a pale linen suit, strode into the room. He bowed to both women and lifted Talia's hand and kissed it, his eyes locked with hers. 'Forgive my intrusion. I was watching when you left the terrace and saw Alexei race after you with some of his men. I could not leave until I knew all was well with you,' he told her, in a voice exactly like his son's.

A delicate flush rose in Talia's face as she freed her hand. 'This is a surprise, Milo. What are you doing here?'

'It is our son's birthday, is it not?'

Alex made a hostile move, but at a look from his mother he backed off.

'A card would have done, Milo,' she observed, in a tone so sweet and cold it sent shivers down Eleanor's spine.

He surveyed her bleakly. 'Instead I came to mingle with the crowds, hoping to give my wishes myself. To my surprise, I was granted the unexpected privilege of seeing you here, Talia, and so I stayed, even knowing I risked instant ejection from my son's island if he saw me.'

'Of course I saw you,' grated Alex. 'But throwing you off Kyrkiros would have attracted unwelcome attention to my mother.'

Eleanor got to her feet hastily. 'If you'll excuse me, I'll say goodnight.'

'Goodnight, my dear.' Talia smiled at her son. 'Escort Eleanor to your room, please, Alexei *mou*.'

In silence so thick it seemed to drain the oxygen from the air, Alex led Eleanor along the hall to his own bedroom, his reluctance to leave his parents alone together coming off him like gamma rays.

'I hope you'll be comfortable in here,' he said stiffly as he ushered her into a starkly masculine bedroom so unlike Talia's it could have been in a different building.

'I'm sorry to turn you out of your room,' she said, equally stiff.

He shrugged. 'In the circumstances, the least I can do. But I must collect some belongings before I leave you to the rest you must be desperate for by now.' He looked back along the hall, his jaw clenched. 'I apologise. I should have introduced you back there.'

'I recognised your father from his photograph.'

'Of course you did. You're a reporter.'

'Yes. I am.' Eleanor sighed wearily. 'And, before you ask, I won't mention Milo Drakis in my article either.'

'Thank you.' To her surprise, Alex actually smiled. 'Keeping the lid on all this drama must be hellish frustrating for you.'

'True. But to avoid any hurt to your mother I'll make do with a colourful account of the festival and say nothing about the rest.'

'Even though someone tried to drown you?' For the first time his eyes held a touch of warmth. 'I hope this paper you work for pays you well. You earned danger money today.'

Her lips twitched. 'According to my editor, I get money for old rope. He calls this kind of assignment a paid holiday.'

'Not quite the way it went down today!' He crossed to a wardrobe and looked over his shoulder. 'Help yourself to a T-shirt, or whatever, to sleep in.'

The intimacy of the situation put Eleanor on edge as Alex went into the bathroom.

'Tomorrow night,' he said when he emerged, 'You can sleep in my mother's room.'

She stared at him in surprise. 'I thought you were hustling me back to the UK tomorrow.'

He shrugged irritably. 'I was, but while you were getting cleaned up earlier my mother pointed out that you should be allowed to enjoy the rest of your holiday as planned. I can't guarantee your safety on Karpyros, but I can if you stay on here. You'd have Sofia to look after you and give you meals, and Theo Lazarides for security. You can have the run of the place, other than my office, and if you find the Kastro too intimidating to sleep in alone I can ask Sofia to move up here until you leave.'

'Why are you doing this?' she asked, astonished.

A flash of respect lit the dark eyes. 'I owe you, Ms Markham. You risked your own safety, even your life, to help my mother today. I pride myself on paying my debts. Or do you have a different reward in mind?'

She nodded. 'Actually, I do, but I'll let your

mother fill you in on that. Right now, I'm so tired I can hardly keep my eyes open.'

He hesitated, and then surprised her by shaking her hand briefly. 'Thank you again, Eleanor Markham. Goodnight.'

'Goodnight.' She watched the door close behind him, wishing she could be a fly on the wall when he re-joined his parents.

Instead of doing so immediately, Alexei Drakos went into the tower room to stare out at the night sky, his mind more occupied with Eleanor than his parents who, much as he hated to admit it, were probably both pleased to be left alone together for a while. Besides, they were not his immediate problem—unlike the woman occupying his bedroom tonight.

He shook his head impatiently. He'd obviously gone too long without the pleasure of a woman to warm his bed. Since the degrading business with Christina, he'd avoided all women, which meant that part of Eleanor Markham's appeal was her appearance in his life at a time of sexual drought. But the bright eyes in that narrow face had caught his eye this afternoon, otherwise he wouldn't have offered his help. The discovery that she was a journalist had been like a punch to the ribs.

He winced. It was she who had taken that kind of blow tonight, in her fight to save his mother. No getting away from it, damn it. He owed her. He turned away abruptly, squaring his shoulders. Time to knock on his mother's bedroom door and politely request that his father leave. God, what a night!

CHAPTER THREE

ELEANOR woke next morning to a knock on the door, and for a moment stared blankly at her surroundings. She heaved herself up in Alexei Drakos' vast bed, wincing as her various bruises came to life.

Sofia backed in with a tray, smiling. '*Kalimera, kyria.*'

Eleanor returned the greeting, and asked after Talia.

'*Kyria* Talia has gone, but she left you this.' Sofia took a letter from her apron pocket. 'She told me to see you rest. Eat well,' she added as she went out.

Eleanor tore open the envelope quickly.

My Dear Eleanor,
I looked in on you earlier but you were so deeply asleep I did not disturb you. Our intruder is now on his way to police custody but

my son insists on escorting me on the ferry to Crete to catch my plane. On the voyage I shall ask him to give you your interview. Enjoy your stay on Kyrkiros. Alex is returning there later, so make sure he gives you your reward for your bravery last night.

Please contact me at the address and telephone numbers above when you get back. In all the excitement, I forgot to ask for yours, and I would so much like to see you again, Eleanor.
With my grateful thanks,
Talia.

Eleanor folded the letter very thoughtfully and turned her attention to the tray. She was hungry, and not even the thought of Alexei Drakos returning to play hell about an interview spoiled her enjoyment of orange juice, rolls warm from the oven and all the coffee in the pot. When Sofia returned she escorted Eleanor to the immaculate guest bedroom, where Eleanor's clothes, including canvas deck shoes, were now dry and ready to wear.

Eleanor thanked the woman warmly, and asked when *kyrie* Alexei was returning.

Sofia looked puzzled. 'He is not returning here from Crete, *kyria*. But you are to stay as long as you wish.'

Eleanor washed her bitter disappointment away in the shower. So there would be no interview with Alexei Drakos after all. Get over it, she told herself irritably. Comfortable again in her own clothes—other than the canvas flats, which seemed to have shrunk a size after their dunking—she made for the lift and took it down to ground level. Voices led her along the hall to a vast kitchen where Sofia was drinking coffee with two other women.

'*Kalimera*,' Eleanor said in general greeting, and received warm smiles in response. She was introduced to buxom Irene and thin Chloe, both of whom, as far as she could make out, praised her for her bravery of the night before.

'You saved *kyria* Talia,' stated Sofia, and scowled venomously. 'The dog has gone with the police. Did he hurt you?'

Eleanor patted her ribs. 'His foot,' she explained,

illustrating with a kick. 'When he pushed me in the water.'

'You could have died!' exclaimed Irene with drama.

Eleanor shook her head. '*Kyrie* Drakos saved me.' Not that it had been necessary. She could swim well enough. She smiled hopefully. 'Could someone take me over to Karpyros now, please?' If Alexei Drakos wasn't coming back here was no point in hanging around. Besides, her belongings were back in the *taverna,* and she needed her laptop to get some work done.

'Yannis will take you after you eat,' Sofia said firmly. 'I will bring lunch to the tower room.'

Taking this as her cue, Eleanor left the kitchen and went up in the lift to spend a long time gazing at the spectacularly beautiful view of vine-clad slopes rising from cobalt-blue sea before she settled down to make notes about the day before. She sighed in frustration as she wrote, wishing she could spice the account up with details of the bungled kidnap. But even without it the article on Kyrkiros would be the most interesting one of the series, partly because of the photographs she'd taken of the bull dance and partly because the island was owned by Alexei Drakos. He could hardly object if *his* name was mentioned. It would have been common knowledge to everyone at the festival. She was hard at work when Sofia arrived with a tempting asparagus salad.

'Eat well, *kyria,*' said Sofia. 'When you have finished, Yannis will take you over to Karpyros and wait as long as you wish until you are ready to return.'

Eleanor explained, as well as she could with her limited vocabulary, that she was not returning, that she would stay at the *taverna* there until she flew home to England.

This news brought heated protests but in the end the woman left her to her meal and departed, making it plain she disapproved of the change of plan. The *kyrie* would not be pleased.

Pleasing Alexei Drakos was pretty low on Eleanor's list of priorities now there was no chance of an interview. She finished her lunch, collected her bag and went down in the lift to the kitchen, where she delighted the women by asking to take photographs of them, both in the kitchen and outside in the sun with the Kastro as a backdrop. And, when Yannis came to transport the *kyria*,

Eleanor took shots of the youth with his beaming mother.

'I shall send the photographs to you when I get home,' she promised, and followed Yannis down to the main jetty, feeling regret at leaving Kyrkiros, if only for failing to get her interview.

Eleanor was touched by her reception back at the *taverna*, where Takis and Petros informed her that until receiving her message they had been very anxious about her the night before. She explained as well as she could about her lack of mobile phone, and when she reached her small, blessedly private apartment she sat in the sun for a while on the veranda and looked out over the harbour towards Kyrkiros. So much had happened since leaving the room to go over to the island, it was amazing to realise that only a day had elapsed. Suddenly Eleanor thought of her camera. She went inside to check it, and heaved a sigh of relief to find it was still in full working order as she transferred the photographs of the festival to her laptop.

Her first shots of the Kastro and the village houses were good, but the true colour and animation of the day came through with her capture of the festival mood as laughing, chattering tourists toured the stalls for souvenirs. She lingered when she came to the shots she'd taken of Alexei and his mother. In one he was looking down at Talia with a tenderness which gave Eleanor a pang of emotion hard to identify as she went on with the rest of her slideshow. She crowed in jubilation over shots of the torch-lit stage and the bull dancers, who looked even more unreal on the screen, as though she'd flung open a window on the prehistoric past and captured the moment on film.

The money shots were those of the Minotaur when he first burst onto the stage, and Theseus with golden double-axe held aloft. There was also something very special about the sight of the Minotaur borne off the stage on the shoulders of his conquerors. Perhaps her efforts would console Ross McLean for her failure to get an interview with Alexei Drakos. And pigs might fly! Eleanor shrugged philosophically and settled down to write the article that would round off her series.

Due to his mother's inevitable refusal to make the journey in his helicopter, Alexei had been obliged to take the ferry to Crete to see her onto the plane, and spent most of the trip promising her he would take more time in future to relax and enjoy life. It was a wrench, as always, to part with her; and on the way back he occupied himself with calls to Athens and London. For the remainder of the trip he leaned against the rail, calling himself all kinds of fool for letting his mother cajole him into returning to Kyrkiros to babysit a journalist. And, not only a journalist, but one he had fleetingly suspected of involvement in his mother's kidnap. And because Talia rarely asked anything of him—not even more of his company, which he well knew she wanted most of all—he would do as she wanted. It would do him good, he was assured, to get away from it all for a while, in the company of an intelligent, attractive woman who, she pointedly reminded him, he was indebted to for his mother's safety. All Eleanor wanted by way of appreciation was an in-depth interview, Talia had informed him, which had to be a refreshing change from the usual women in his life, who probably demanded very different rewards for their company at his dinner table and or bed...

Alex frowned, wondering exactly what Ms Markham meant by 'in-depth' for the interview.

If she imagined he would lay his soul bare, she was mistaken. Only a fool would do that with anyone, least of all a journalist—even one as appealing as Eleanor. He might be many things, and not all of them admirable, but a fool wasn't one of them. Christina Mavros' malicious spin on their brief affair had been merely a fleeting embarrassment. His hostility towards reporters had begun long before then. From the day he'd found the online accounts of his parents' divorce, the press had been irrevocably linked in his mind with the shattering discovery that his father, his hero, had hurt his mother badly enough to make her divorce him. The hero had crashed from his pedestal and from that day on Milo Drakos' efforts to maintain a normal relationship with his son had met with little success.

When Alex had questioned his mother about the reasons for the divorce, he was told it was something private between her and his father. Talia had refused to say another word, but his grandfather, Cyrus Kazan, had been more forthcoming. If Alex was old enough to ask the question, he was old enough to cope with the answer, had been his grandfather's justification for telling the boy that Milo, though madly in love with his wife, was so insanely jealous he had refused to believe that the child was actually his.

'The problem,' Talia had explained years later when Alex demanded the truth, 'Was the inconvenient fact that I grew large very early on in the pregnancy, which aroused Milo's suspicions. When you were born exactly ten months from our wedding day, Milo was desperately repentant and begged my forgiveness. I'll spare you the details, but it was a long, difficult labour and, because I was exhausted and at the mercy of my hormones, and so furious and heartbroken at his lack of trust, I refused to listen to him. My father, of course, had been ready to kill Milo, but my mother persuaded him to calm down. She pointed out that the best revenge would be to collect Milo's wife and son from the hospital to drive them to the Kazan family home, which would then be barred against him.'

Alex's face was grim as he watched the water streaming past. In the clash between his father and mother it had been a classic case of Greek meeting Greek, which probably explained Talia's vengeance. But, although she was a fiercely protective mother, she was also a practical one determined for the best for her son. Because Milo could provide the best, she had given him the right to have the child baptised Alexei Drakos, rather than Kazan, her original intention.

Milo had also demanded the right to provide for his son's expensive education, with the stipulation that Alex made regular visits to him in Athens and his holiday home on Corfu. When the boy was young these were experiences eagerly anticipated by both father and son. After the shock of his grandfather's revelations, teenage Alex still kept to the agreed visits to his father because his mother was adamant that he should, but he spent most of his time there either swimming in the pool in Corfu, or in Athens glued to the latest thing in computers Milo had bought his son in an effort to win the hostile boy's approval.

Thus began Alex's early passion for technology, which in time led to his development of innovative software which made him a fortune. He had still been at the famous British school his father had insisted on mainly, Alex knew, to prevent him from becoming a 'mother's boy' as Milo feared would happen if his son was left to grow up with only female supervision once old Cyrus died. But Alexei had a parting gift ready for his father during their final holiday together. Due to a stomach bug he left Corfu after only a few days, and at the airport handed Milo a cheque which covered the full amount expended on his education over the years. 'Now I owe you nothing,' he told his father, and left Milo standing stricken as his son boarded the plane. These days Alex felt more regret than satisfaction at the memory, and quickly shut it out by contacting Theo Lazarides to say he was about to dock.

Eleanor was so deeply immersed in her article she almost jumped out of her skin when someone hammered on her door. She flung it open and stared in shock into the dark and angry eyes of Alexei Drakos.

'What the hell are you doing here?' he demanded, his accent more pronounced than usual.

'I might ask the same of you,' she retorted. 'You frightened the life out of me.'

'I damn well hope I did. You threw open the door without even checking to see who it was. After what happened last night are you mad, woman?' He glared at her. 'I rang Theo Laza-rides when I was on the ferry and he said you'd gone. Why the devil didn't you stay on Kyrkiros as arranged?'

'Once the intruder was in custody it was unnec-essary.' Eleanor's chin lifted. 'In any case, why are *you* here? Sofia told me you weren't coming back to Kyrkiros.'

He shrugged impatiently. 'That was the origi-nal plan before all the melodrama yesterday. But after sorting everything with the police, and the rush to get my mother over to the ferry on time this morning, I forgot to tell Sofia I was returning to the island for a while after all. Look,' he added more reasonably, 'Must we discuss this outside? Let me in.'

Eleanor shook her head. 'I think not.'

He made a visible effort to control his temper. '*Why* not?'

Her chin lifted. 'Because you're angry with me.'

Alexei closed his eyes for a moment, as though praying for patience. When he opened them again he stepped back a fraction and raised his hands. 'Ms Markham—Eleanor—I come in peace. I have no intention of harming you in any way. I'm here to take you back to Kyrkiros to make sure you come to no further harm than you've already suffered. There I can keep you safe. Here it is impossible. My mother would never forgive me if anything happened to you that I could have prevented.'

Eleanor frowned, perplexed. 'But I don't need to be kept safe now the kidnapper's locked up.'

'The man who hired him is still out there.' His mouth tightened.

'Look, Mr Drakos...'

He raised a mocking eyebrow. 'It's a bit late for formality!'

She shrugged. 'Alexei, then.'

'Alex.'

'I have a much simpler solution to the problem—Alex.'

'Which is?'

'I forget the holiday and catch the first possible flight home.'

Alex gave her an unsettling smile. 'But if you do that you'll go without your reward. My mother told me—in great detail—what you want, and persuaded me to agree. So to achieve your ambition, Eleanor Markham, you must stay on for a while.'

Her heart leapt. He really meant to give her an interview? She moved back at the sound of people approaching the other apartments. 'You'd better come in.'

'Thank you.' Alex stepped inside, an eyebrow raised as she closed the door. 'Why the change of heart?'

'The possibility of an interview was worth the risk,' she said bluntly.

'You're not at risk from me, Eleanor.'

'Good to know.' She waved him to the couch. 'Do sit down.'

'No time for that. I want you to come with me right now. I'll sort Takis out.'

'Certainly not. *If* I decide to come, I'll do that myself.' Eleanor gave him an assessing look as she considered the pros and cons of a stay on Kyrkiros. 'You would really give me an interview?'

'With certain subjects off-limits, yes.' He smiled cynically. 'Your editor would be pleased.'

'Ecstatic,' she agreed, resigned. 'But I still can't see why I have to stay on Kyrkiros to do it. Why would anyone bother about me now your mother's gone home?'

'You were seen on the island, sharing my table in company with her. You are therefore perceived as important to me.' Alex's eyes hardened. 'From a ransom angle the attempt on my mother failed, so you're the next best thing.' He thrust a hand through his hair. 'Besides, I have a gut feeling that you're in danger. Laugh if you want, but I've been subject to feelings like this at times all my life. I've learned the hard way not to ignore them.'

'Premonitions, you mean?'

'Not exactly. The nearest explanation I can give is the electricity in the air before a storm breaks. And, though the weather's set fair, I'm feeling it on the back of my neck right now. So for God's sake pack your bags and let's get out of here.'

The promise of an interview decided Eleanor. She saved her work on the laptop, stuffed her notebook and camera into her tote bag and went up the ladder at top speed to pack the rest of her belongings.

'I must take the key to Takis,' she told Alex as she handed the bags down to him.

'The ferry to Crete is about to leave. Tell him you've changed your mind and you're catching it. I moored my boat well out of sight of the *taverna* this morning when I brought my mother over, so with luck we can get away unseen.'

The enormity of what she was doing suddenly struck Eleanor full force. 'I must be mad! My phone is broken, and I'm taking off with a virtual stranger without telling anyone where I'm going. I could disappear off the face of the earth with no one the wiser.'

Alex gritted his teeth. 'I can tell you write for a living! Plan B, then. I'll get Takis over here so that you can tell him where you're going and I'll swear him to silence to keep you safe. I'll speak slowly so you understand me. Deal?'

She nodded reluctantly. 'Deal.'

'Good. Lock the door behind me and stay inside until I come back.'

Eleanor waited, her belongings at her feet, not sure whether she was setting out on an adventure or making the worst mistake of her life. But it was worth the risk to get the interview. And hopefully Alex would see that she got to Crete to catch her plane home afterwards. Any other journalist would be jumping for joy, and professionally she was. But on a personal level she had serious reservations about spending time with a hostile man who was only suffering her company to ensure her safety—and even then only because his mother had used emotional blackmail to get him to agree.

Alex returned quickly with Takis and ushered the *taverna* owner into the room. 'Right then, Eleanor. Muster your best Greek and explain to him yourself.'

Eleanor felt awkward as she told Takis she was leaving with *kyrie* Drakos to stay on his island. But when Alex explained the kidnap threat to him, slowly and clearly so she could understand, the man's kindly face darkened and he swore that they could trust him to say nothing. He advised them to go down to the boat via the little-used path beyond Eleanor's apartment, and thus avoid passing any curious eyes at the *taverna*s along the harbour.

There was no lighting on the path. It was both narrow and steep, but Alex kept up a punishing pace in silence on the way down to the harbour. When Eleanor, gasping for breath, was finally sitting amongst her belongings in the stern of a sleek boat, the engine noise was too loud to ask questions. She felt a surge of alarm when she found

Alex was taking a much longer route than her trip the day before but eventually calmed down, embarrassed, when she realised he'd merely made a wide detour around the island to a mooring behind the Kastro. When a man appeared from the quayside buildings to secure the boat, Alex jumped up onto the dimly lit jetty and leaned down to take Eleanor's luggage, before helping her out.

'This is my private dock, and this is Theo Lazarides, who takes care of security here. Ms Markham will be staying here for a few days, Theo.'

'Welcome back, Ms Markham,' he said politely.

She smiled. '*Efcharisto, kyrie* Lazarides.'

Alex picked up the luggage and Eleanor took charge of her tote bag and laptop. 'Let's get inside.' He looked at Theo. 'Has everyone been warned?'

'Yes, *kyrie*.'

With a brisk nod Alex shifted both bags to one hand, and took hold of Eleanor's arm with the other. 'Careful, it's a rough surface along here and there are no lights. I keep it that way on purpose.'

'To repel intruders?'

'More or less, though until now we've never had

any. The man you had the bad luck to run into last night is the first since I took the place over. But he was just someone's tool, so vigilance is now doubly necessary. Careful,' he added as she stumbled.

Infected with Alex's urgency, Eleanor felt safe only when they came in range of the lights from the Kastro and entered the old citadel from the back via a passageway with several more doors opening off it. Alex dumped the bags and locked the outer door behind them, then took her to Sofia in the kitchen.

The woman smiled warmly as she welcomed Eleanor back. 'I will take you to your room.'

'I'll do that, Sofia,' said Alex quickly, and added a lot more that Eleanor couldn't understand.

'What were you telling her?' she demanded as they went up in the lift.

'Merely that we would both need time for baths before we eat.' Alex gave her a sardonic smile as the doors opened. 'Was that imagination of yours at work again, cooking up something sinister?'

'No.' Eleanor shrugged. 'I just get frustrated when I don't understand what's going on, so make allowances, please.'

'I could give you lessons,' he offered, surprising her.

'I won't be here long enough for that. But thank you,' she added, and smiled politely as she went into the bedroom ahead of him. 'In fact, thank you for a lot more than that. I'm very conscious that I'm keeping you from returning to Athens.'

Alex put her bags down on the chaise at the foot of the bed and turned to look at her very directly. 'I can spare a few days. Stefan is already back there, and I can keep in contact with him and everyone else in the world I need to from my office right here in the *Kastro*.'

'You like to be in control,' said Eleanor, making mental notes. 'I did some research on you before I came.'

'Of course you did,' he said, lips tightening. 'And what did you learn, Eleanor? Colourful details about my private life?'

She looked at him very directly. 'You know perfectly well there aren't many.'

He looked sceptical. 'You must have found the account of my private life by one Christina Mavros!'

'Yes, but I dismissed that as sheer "woman

scorned" invective. I also read about your parents' divorce and that your mother was one of the most beautiful photographic models of her generation. But other than Miss Mavros's nasty little piece I found very little, except that you were a boy genius who achieved success very young.'

'Oh, I was clever enough,' he said harshly. 'But my first taste of British public school was hell—' He broke off with a curse. 'That's strictly off the record. I'll give you a formal interview tomorrow. In the meantime, have a rest or bath or whatever before dinner, which will be in an hour or so. I'll knock when it arrives.'

'Thank you.' Eleanor's eyes were thoughtful as she closed the door behind him. He need have no worries about her discretion. Having achieved the impossible dream of an interview with Alexei Drakos, there was no way she would risk having him set lawyers on her by writing anything he would object to seeing in print.

After a shower, Eleanor rolled her dress in a ball and stuffed it in one of her bags. Sophia's careful laundering had done wonders but she would never wear it again. She shrugged. Alex might be accustomed to women in designer finery at his dinner table, but tonight he would have to put up with a guest in jeans and one of a dwindling supply of clean T-shirts. On the bright side, a touch of make-up and a spritz of perfume was a definite improvement on the drowned-rat look of the night before, especially if she left her hair down. No curls, but there was a lot of it—shiny as chocolate sauce, according to one old flame—and her shoulder-skimming bob was still in good shape, courtesy of the haircut she had splashed out on before leaving home.

She sent a message to her parents via her laptop, but took a paperback out of her holdall instead of getting down to work. She climbed up on the pretty white bed to settle against the pillows, and sighed with pleasure at the thought of reading something that wasn't research. And, after days of hopping on and off ferries to go in search of various accommodations she'd organised herself, it was rather good to feel all responsibility had now been taken out of her hands until she flew home.

When she heard the expected knock, Eleanor put a bookmark in her novel and got off the bed to thrust her feet into yellow canvas espadrilles in place of the shrunken navy flats. 'Come in.'

Alex put his head round the door. 'I thought we'd have a drink before the meal.'

'Thank you.'

He smiled briefly as she joined him in the hall. 'I see we both had the same idea about dressing down tonight.'

'Not much choice for me. I packed only two dresses.'

'You look just as good in jeans,' he said casually, with a look which sent a jolt of unwelcome heat through her. 'We have no one here to impress, so after all the drama yesterday the priority tonight is comfort. I hope you *are* comfortable with me, Eleanor?'

She sat down in a corner of the sofa, thinking it over. 'I will be eventually.'

'But not yet?'

'I hardly know you,' she pointed out. 'We're strangers, after all.'

'Yet you were at ease with my mother right from the first.'

Eleanor smiled. 'She's a very special lady.'

'True.' His eyes softened. 'I was the envy of my friends when she came to prize days and cricket matches. She bought a house in Berkshire within easy travelling distance of the school when I first started there, and my grandfather flew over to accompany her as often as he could so I wouldn't feel out of it when other boys had fathers to cheer them on.' He eyed her quizzically. 'Your research didn't turn up mention of Cyrus Kazan?'

'No.' Eleanor held her breath, astonished that she was hearing personal details of Alexei Drakos' life.

'What would you like to drink?' he asked. 'A cocktail or some of this wine?'

'Wine, please,' she said, willing him to go on about his family.

'It comes from vineyards here on the island. Under my friend Dion Aristides' expert guiding hand, most of it is exported these days— part of my ongoing development programme for Kyrkiros.' Alex filled two glasses and sat down beside her.

'After the festival yesterday orders will be flooding in,' said Eleanor, tasting with pleasure. 'It's really excellent. But surely you would do even better if you opened the island to visitors more often?'

'It depends on what you mean by better. At present supply keeps pace with demand. Expansion would mean a bigger workforce we've no room to house. As things stand, the export of wine, olives and various crafts made by the islanders keeps the population in steady income throughout the year to augment the living from fishing. The quality of life is good here.'

'I'd love to explore your island,' she said hopefully.

He shook his head. 'In normal circumstances I would be glad to show you, but after the drama of getting you here that would be counterproductive.'

'But surely the islanders will know I'm here?'

'Of course. But Theo has made sure no one talks to outsiders.' Alex eyed her narrowly. 'You don't look happy.'

Eleanor smiled ruefully. 'I hate to sound ungrateful, but after my travels I'd really looked forward to lazing around on a beach for a while before flying home.'

'Tomorrow I'll show you a place where you can sunbathe to your heart's content in complete privacy.' He got up as Sofia and Yannis arrived with a serving trolley, the former voluble with apologies she addressed to Alex at such speed Eleanor soon gave up trying to understand.

Alex held up a hand, laughing, and translated for Eleanor. 'Sofia thought I was leaving today and apologises for serving such simple food tonight. Tomorrow she will do better.'

Eleanor sniffed at the appetising aromas coming from the trolley and assured Sofia that it all smelled delicious.

'Eat well to recover strength,' said the woman, slowly and deliberately this time so Eleanor could understand.

'*Efcharisto.*' Eleanor included Yannis in her smile as the pair left.

'As you can probably tell,' said Alex, 'Sofia, like everyone else on the island, was impressed by your bravery last night. We are instructed to eat the cold dish first,' he added, and seated her at the table under the window before sitting opposite her.

Eleanor mentally raised an eyebrow as she transferred stuffed aubergines to their plates. Alexei obviously took it for granted she would serve him.

'I would have asked Sofia to stay to serve the

meal,' he said, apparently reading her mind, 'But I thought you might prefer less formality.'

'You were right.' She tasted the aubergine's spicy tomato filling. 'This is very good. On my travels I've kept to fish and salad mostly.'

'You don't eat meat?'

'I do, but in some places goat was on the menu, and my courage failed!'

He laughed. 'You're safe tonight. I'm told the *entrée* features pork.'

Eleanor felt like pinching herself from time to time as she ate, to be sure she really was dining with Alexei Drakos. She'd been bowled over by his charisma from the first, so deeply attracted to him on sight his threats had been a bitter blow. But right now, instead of enduring her company politely as she'd expected, he was pulling out all the stops to put her at ease. And to be fair he was really something to look at now his hair, damp from a shower earlier on, had dried to a sun-streaked gold halo. Well, maybe not a halo. This man was no saint.

'Is a penny enough for your thoughts?' he said abruptly, and smiled slowly as a wave of scarlet flooded her face. 'Obviously not!'

'This is all so unreal,' she said, going for part of the truth. 'When I came to the island to report on the festival I never thought for a minute that you would speak to me at all, let alone agree to an interview.'

'You can thank my mother for that. She asked me to give you the reward you asked for, and because we are both indebted to you I will do so. But,' he stated with emphasis, 'I will personally check every word of the article when it's finished. And if and when I'm satisfied it must go off before you leave.'

'By all means. You can stand over me while I press Send!'

Alex raised a cynical eyebrow. 'And how do I know your editor will print it exactly as it stands? He could apply his own spin and make something completely different out of it.'

'I'll give you his email address so you can hit him with the threats you made to me. Believe me; Ross McLean will do whatever you want to get his exclusive.' Eleanor took their plates to the trolley and returned with the hot *entrée* dishes. She set them on the table and handed Alex a pair of large serving spoons. 'There you go.'

'Ah! I obviously took your help for granted earlier.'

'Not a problem.' Eleanor smiled demurely. 'I'm grateful to you for the food I'm eating, whoever serves it.'

Alex shook his head in sorrow as he filled their plates. 'A beautiful woman is sharing a meal with me and feels only gratitude?'

'Not at all.' And wasn't that the truth. 'As I said before, I feel the unlikeliness of it too.'

He laughed. 'Nevertheless here we are, sharing a meal as men and women do everywhere. But in return for this supper you're so grateful for, *kyria* journalist, you must sing for it. Tell me more about Eleanor Markham.'

She eyed him challengingly. 'I will if you return the compliment.'

'I have promised to do so!'

'But that will be an interview with Alexei Drakos, the public figure, with every word I write subject to your approval.' She smiled persuasively. 'I'd like to know more about the private man. Strictly off the record, of course.'

He gave her a hard look. 'No notebook or camera?'

She shook her head. 'Just my sworn oath to tell no one. Ever.'

Alex concentrated on slow-cooked pork of melting tenderness for a moment or two. 'I'm not in the habit of discussing my personal life with anyone, least of all a journalist.'

'Forget I'm a journalist. Just think of me as a woman,' Eleanor said promptly.

His eyes moved over her in deliberation which sent her pulse up a gear. 'Impossible to do otherwise,' he assured her. 'Very well, Eleanor Markham. You give me your life story and I'll respond with some of mine.'

'Some?'

'That's the deal.'

'Done.' She got up, serving spoons in hand. 'In that case, I'll help you to more of this delicious meal.'

When he threw back his head and laughed Eleanor's heart did a quick forward roll against her sore ribs. 'You're happy to wait on me now.'

'Absolutely.'

'Then I accept. And now you talk.' He filled their glasses and looked at her expectantly.

Eleanor topped up his plate and resumed her

chair. 'There's not much to tell,' she began, wishing there were. 'My career began with a Saturday job on a local newspaper when I was a schoolgirl. I was offered a full-time job there later, but went to university instead. I graduated with a respectable English degree, worked hard to add qualifications in journalism and photography to go with it and gained experience with various newspapers before my present job.' She looked up to meet the intent dark eyes. 'That's it, really.'

'For a writer, there's very little human interest in your story, Eleanor. Where are the tales of wild student parties and the men in your life?' he demanded.

She sighed. 'In my past, regretfully.'

Alex eyed her thoughtfully as he drained his glass. 'All of them?'

'The ones from the wild student days, yes.'

'How about in the present?'

'As I told your mother, my job is hard on personal relationships. But I have good friends so the drawback doesn't bother me too much.' She pulled a face. 'Compared with your life mine sounds numbingly dull.'

'Not recently,' he reminded her, and picked up

her hand to examine her bruised knuckles. 'It was anything but when that reprobate kicked you into the sea last night.'

Eleanor agreed with a shiver which had more to do with his touch than the incident. 'I haven't thanked you properly for rescuing me—though when you first grabbed me I thought it was the man, trying to drown me for real.'

'It was like trying to rescue an eel!' he agreed and eyed her quizzically. 'But did you really need rescuing?'

'No. I'm a fairly strong swimmer. Once I made it to the surface, I could have swum back to the jetty easily enough. Well, maybe not easily. The wretch hurt me quite a bit.'

'Which is why I dived in after you. When you'd just laid into my mother's kidnapper it was the least I could do.'

'And much appreciated,' said Eleanor and sat back. 'Your turn now.'

He leaned over to refill her glass. 'What do you want to know?'

'Anything you care to tell me. Perhaps I could just ask some questions? It's entirely up to you whether you answer them.'

'If you wish,' said Alex, resigned.

'Can we go back to the time when you started in prep school? Why was it such hell?'

He was silent for some time, wondering why it felt so easy to confide in her, when normally he refused to talk about himself to anyone at all other than his mother, and even then only rarely. 'To admit this is very bad for my image, but at first I missed my mother so much I buried my face in the pillow every night so no one heard me cry. I was a pretty average size at that age, and cursed with this hair. I could speak English fluently enough, due to tutors my father employed to prepare me for the new school, but I spoke it with an accent—as I still do. When the rugby season started, things looked up. In the front row of the pack in a scrum I learned a few tricks—not all of them in the rule book—which were a great help. I put on a burst of growth, grew taller very quickly, did well at other sports and life became bearable.'

'How old were you when you went away to school?'

'Too young,' Alex said without inflection.

Eleanor eyed him with compassion, picturing a little boy with golden curls crying at night for his mother. 'I didn't go away to school, at least not until I went to university, so by the time I flew the nest I was raring to go.'

'A much better arrangement.' He shrugged. 'But, hard though school was in the beginning, I made good friends there in time, including the master who opened up the world of technology to me.'

'I read that you made a fortune from it while you were still in school.'

Alex shrugged. 'I have two people to thank for that: my grandfather, who put up the money to back me on my venture, and my father.'

Eleanor stared at him in surprise.

'Milo Drakos bought me the latest and most expensive computer to play with every time I went to stay with him.' He smiled grimly. 'This only stopped when I refused to go there any more.'

'He gave up buying expensive bribes?'

'No. He became involved with a woman who hated me.' He shot her a look. 'Surely your research turned up that bit of information?'

'No, it didn't. Is your father still involved with her?'

Alex shook his head. 'The relationship was

short-lived, because the lady not only objected to my visits but demanded that he marry her and adopt her son from a former marriage; a huge mistake on her part.' The dark eyes hardened. 'She had no hope of it anyway. It annoys the hell out of me to admit it, but I'm sure Milo's still in love with my mother.'

Eleanor could well believe it. The electricity in the air had fairly crackled when Milo Drakos had walked into his ex-wife's bedroom the night before. 'May I ask how she feels about him?' she said carefully.

'I can't tell you. If I bring the subject up she refuses to discuss it. My beautiful mother may look sweet and malleable, but she has a will of iron, and pride to match.' He broke off at a knock on the door and smiled at Sofia as she came in to put a coffee tray on a table in front of the sofa.

'The meal was delicious,' Eleanor told her.

'*Efcharisto*,' said the woman, pleased, and began clearing the dinner table. 'Do you need anything else, *kyrie?*' she asked Alex.

He shook his head. 'Nothing more tonight.'

She wished them both good night and went out with the trolley.

'Yannis didn't come back with her,' said Eleanor. 'Does she live nearby?'

'Right here in the *Kastro*, in a ground floor apartment adjoining the kitchen.'

'She's a widow?'

Alex nodded soberly. 'When her husband died a year or so after I took over the island I offered her the job of housekeeper, with rooms in the *Kastro* for her and the boy.' He gestured towards the sofa. 'Let's move over there.' He smiled blandly. 'Perhaps you'd even pour my coffee.'

Eleanor grinned at him. 'My pleasure!'

Alex shot her a probing glance as they sat down. 'Do you feel happier now you know that Sofia and Yannis sleep in the building?'

She stared at him in surprise. 'No. I wasn't unhappy before.'

'So you really do believe I mean you no harm.'

'It never occurred to me to think otherwise.' She paused. 'I assume Sofia is accustomed to catering for guests?'

Alex gave her a smile which transformed his face from merely handsome to off-the-charts breath-taking. 'If that's a way of asking whether I bring a lot of women here, the ladies I know are city dwellers who demand venues more sophisticated than a remote island lacking even a *taverna*. Besides, this place is my retreat. And, if you're worried about the proprieties, your deeds yesterday ensure that your reputation can survive a couple of nights alone here with me.' He reached for the coffee pot and refilled their cups. 'Tell me more about yourself and the life you lead.'

CHAPTER FOUR

ELEANOR shook her head. 'I'd much rather talk about Alexei Drakos.'

He raised a dark eyebrow. 'You had no trouble in talking about yourself to my mother.'

'That's different.'

'Because you liked her from the moment you met, whereas you're still not comfortable with me.'

Her eyes flashed. 'Do you blame me? It's not every day I meet a man who threatens me with a lawsuit!'

He shrugged impenitently. 'I will always do everything within my power to protect my mother. And at the time of my threat I'd only just met you. But since then I have compelling reasons to be grateful to you.'

'I see. So when will you give me the interview?'

'In the morning—early, if you wish.'

'I do.' And once she'd written the piece and

Alexei had vetted it she would send it off to Ross McLean and then catch the first possible flight back home. Alex might be the most powerfully attractive man she was ever likely to meet, but she disliked the idea of being marooned here with no way of getting off his island until he agreed to take her to Karpyros to catch the ferry. As soon as he did she would leave whether she could get an earlier flight or not. She could spend the waiting time exploring Crete.

'What are you thinking about now?' he demanded. 'Nothing pleasant, by the look on that expressive face of yours.'

'On the contrary, I'm glad that you're willing to get on with the interview right away.' She smiled politely. 'The moment you approve it I'll send it off and get the ferry to Crete out of your way.'

He raised a dark eyebrow. 'This is rather different from the woman who insisted on a week's holiday. What's changed your mind?'

Her chin lifted. 'On Karpyros I could have left any time I wished. Here I can't.'

Alex frowned. 'You're not a prisoner, Eleanor. The precautions are purely for your own safety. I will take you over to Karpyros early in the morning if you want.' He paused. 'Of course, if you do that you won't get your interview.'

She nodded, resigned. 'Which leaves me with no choice.'

'Exactly.' He got to his feet and held out his hand. 'You're obviously tired. I'll see you to your room.'

She ignored the hand as she got up. 'Thank you. But I don't need an escort.'

'My intention,' he assured her, 'Was to leave you at your door, I swear.'

A wave of heat flooded her face. 'I didn't think otherwise,' she said stiffly, and to her embarrassment gave a sudden yawn.

The eyes that looked so dark under the crown of dark-gold hair glittered with mockery. 'I've offended you and embarrassed the hell out of you, and now I've bored you to death.'

'Absolutely not.' Eleanor smiled sweetly. 'I've been hanging on your every word—as I will tomorrow during the interview.'

'Is that all you can think about—?' He stopped short, eyes narrowed in hostile speculation. 'Is *that* why you tried to rescue my mother? Was the blasted interview so vital you actually risked your life to make me agree to it?'

Eleanor glared at him, incensed. Fists clenched, she turned on her heel and made for the door but he was there before her to open it. She brushed past and hurried ahead of him along the hall to reach his mother's room in time to shut the door in his face.

'Open this door!' Alex called, equally furious, by the sound of him as he hammered on it.

She gave the paintwork a look vitriolic enough to strip it to the bare wood and went into the bathroom to shut out the pounding. It was a good thing Sofia lived out of earshot. She bit her lip, not sure that it was such a good thing after all. She hadn't thought of it before he brought the subject up, but the fact remained that she was alone up here with Alexei Drakos, who was now in a towering rage. She gritted her teeth. He wasn't the only one. She needed another shower to cool off before she could think of bed. She turned on the water and opened the bathroom door a crack. All was quiet. Alex had obviously stormed off to his room, or his office, or wherever.

Eleanor swathed a towel round her head to protect her hair, then stood under a lukewarm shower until she felt calmer. Later, in the camisole and boxers she wore to bed, she leaned back on the bed to read for a while, but soon gave up trying to concentrate. Strange. Alone in the little apartment over on Karpyros, she had felt perfectly safe, but here, locked away at the top of what was virtually a citadel, she felt anything but. Alexei Drakos' fault, damn him.

A quiet knock on the door brought her bolt upright. 'Who is it?'

'Who do you think? Open up, please.'

'Why?'

'I want to speak to you.'

With reluctance Eleanor slid off the bed and pulled on her dressing gown. She opened the door a crack and peered through it.

Alexei Drakos made no attempt to move nearer, but she tensed at the look in his eyes.

'You said you meant me no harm,' she said sharply.

'I don't. But I object to having doors shut in my face in my own home.'

'It was either that or get physically violent. As I did yesterday with the intruder,' she reminded him.

'Quite a temper you lost back there.'

'Do you blame me? You actually accused me of helping your mother just to get an interview!' Her eyes speared his. 'For the record, *kyrie* Drakos, my sole thought was getting her away from the man who snatched her. I was so furious I could have killed him with my bare hands.'

'You had a damned good try,' he agreed, his tone lighter. 'I suppose I must be grateful you slammed the door instead of attempting to murder *me*!' He moved nearer. 'I came to apologise. May I come in?'

With reluctance Eleanor opened the door wider and retreated to sit bolt upright on one of the blue velvet chairs where she'd felt so at ease with Talia Kazan.

Alex eyed her speculatively as he took the other chair. 'Do you feel better now?'

'I'm working on it.'

'I apologise for the crack about the interview.' He laid his hand on his heart. 'I'm sure your motives were of the purest when you went into battle for my mother.'

'Are you?'

'Am I what?'

'Sure.'

He crossed his long legs and sat back, eyeing her objectively. 'Now I've had time to think I am sure, yes. But consider it from my angle—you had only met my mother that day. It was hard to believe you'd put yourself at such risk for a stranger without *some* kind of ulterior motive.'

'I acted on basic gut instinct. Motives didn't come into it. Your mother needed help; I did my best to give it.'

Alex smiled wryly. 'Yet you're no amazon. Our man Spiro refused to believe a woman was responsible for his injuries.'

'He would have had a few more if he hadn't kicked me into the sea!'

'I think the worst part for him was the scorn from Theo Lazarides.' His lips twitched. 'He is deeply impressed by you, Eleanor.'

She shrugged. 'It's nice to know somebody respects me.'

'I do.' Alex leaned forward, hands clasped loosely between his knees. 'Even if the interview *was* part of your motive, I respect a woman willing to go to such lengths to gain her heart's desire.'

'I suppose I take that as an apology.' She smiled sweetly. 'I trust the door incident didn't dent your male hubris too much?'

'It was a new experience. Not one I cared for.' His eyes held hers as he got up. 'I apologise for hammering on the door.'

'For the second time today, if we're counting.'

'I must cure myself of the habit. Tomorrow I promise to be sweetness and light all day.' He smiled sardonically. 'At least I promise to try. Goodnight.'

'Goodnight.'

Alex went out and closed the door behind him. 'Now lock it,' he called as he left, and strode along the hall to his own room when what he really wanted was to go back to Eleanor and take her to bed. Having a door slammed on his face had fired up his libido to the point where he needed a cold shower. He shook his head, baffled. Eleanor appealed to him more than any woman he'd met in a long time, though for the life of him he couldn't say why. Her figure was boyish, and her temperament abrasive, but he wanted her. And since they were alone here, shut away from the world for a day or two, it would be only natural for a man and woman to take the best possible advantage of the situation.

Even with the door securely locked it was a long time before Eleanor went to sleep, and when she did she dreamed about monsters that chased her into the sea. It was a relief to wake to sunlight and the knowledge that today she could get the interview done and be free to go. Powerfully attractive though Alexei Drakos might be, the constant hint of danger about him kept her on edge all the time. Eleanor shrugged irritably and slipped out of bed to unlock the door, ready to admit Sofia with her breakfast, then washed, dressed in denim shorts and one of her dwindling supply of fresh T-shirts and secured her hair back in its pony-tail, ready to get to work.

When the expected knock sounded on her door, Eleanor opened it to find Alex outside, damp of hair and radiating vitality, as though he'd been up for hours.

'*Kalimera*, Eleanor Markham.'

'Good morning,' she said, surprised. 'I was expecting Sofia.'

'I asked her to serve breakfast in the tower room. Will you join me?'

'Thank you, but I don't eat much breakfast,' she warned as she followed him.

'A pity you couldn't have joined me for a swim first to give you an appetite, but in the circumstances it's not advisable. I can provide a pleasant place for the sunbathing you yearned for, but you must keep to a bath for your water fix.' He held out a chair at the table which was laid with hot rolls, fresh fruit and two steaming pots, one of which was tea, he informed her. 'My mother left some of her favourite brand for you.'

'How kind!' Eleanor was struck again by the fantasy aspect of the situation as she faced Alexei Drakos across a breakfast table with a backdrop of sunlit blue Aegean below. After their little altercation of the night before, she had expected him to be hostile; instead he was slaying her with that smile of his. 'It must be wonderful to live in a place like this.'

'I don't live here. Kyrkiros merely serves as

an occasional escape-hatch from life in the real world.'

She smiled. 'Like a kind of holiday home, complete with castle and state-of-the-art office where you can keep tabs on your empire.'

'I do that wherever I am.'

'And Stefan keeps you in touch from Athens?'

'Stefan heads a team there, yes.' He watched her buttering a roll, his eyes amused. 'Shouldn't you be noting this down?'

Eleanor shook her head. 'I'll put my journalist's hat on later when we get down to business.' She picked up the coffee pot and filled his cup.

'Thank you,' he said in mock surprise. 'Are you softening me up to get at all my secrets?'

'Whatever works,' she said cheerfully.

'How long an interview do you want?'

'I'll take all the information you'll give me.'

'It won't be that much,' he warned. 'After you've finished, I'd like to show you something before you get down to work.'

Eleanor smiled hopefully. 'You're going to show me over the *Kastro*?'

He shook his head. 'It's still a work in progress down in the basement area. It was made safe when I first took over here, of course, before the living quarters were done. But I keep to local labour for the renovation work, with fishermen who transform into builders and stone masons in winter when wild winds and rough seas put a stop to fishing, so the progress is slow. Right now I'll show you my garden instead.'

After breakfast Alex led the way along the hall past the bedrooms and the lift, and on round a bend which brought them to the head of the spiral stone staircase ascending from below, with a further short flight leading up to what she thought must be an attic of some kind.

'I'll go first,' he said. 'But be careful, the steps are uneven in places.'

Intrigued, Eleanor kept close behind him. At the top Alex opened a door to let in a glare of sunlight and turned to help her up the last couple of steps.

'Welcome to my secret lair.'

Eleanor gazed in delight at a rooftop garden. Huge terracotta pots overflowing with greenery and flowering plants surrounded a central paved space furnished with chairs and tables shaded by parasols.

'How absolutely lovely.' She smiled as she noticed a screen suspended between two pillars. 'Surely you're not worried about privacy up here?'

Alex shook his head. 'When the *meltemi* blows at the end of summer the screen is very necessary.'

She laughed. 'I can relate. Cowering behind a windbreak on a windy beach was part of the deal on childhood holidays. How about you?'

'I spent my summer holidays at my father's house on Corfu.'

'I remember. You were too busy swimming and sailing and playing with your computer to need windbreaks as we ordinary mortals do.'

'Most ordinary mortals fly off to the sun for their holidays.'

'*Touché*,' she conceded and sat down on one of the reclining chairs. 'My parents were never keen on air travel, so my first holidays abroad were spent with college friends. The travelling was the big attraction in my present job.'

Alex drew up a chair beside her. 'Will your editor give you a promotion when you send him the article?'

She laughed. 'Highly unlikely.'

'I could make it a condition.'

'Absolutely not—thank you.'

'I can at least insist that your name is on the article.'

She thought about it. Her name would be above the travel series as usual, but the Alexei Drakos exclusive was so important to Ross he would want it under his own by-line.

Alex frowned. 'You don't want that either?'

'No, thank you. I don't.' She could just imagine Ross's reaction.

'As you wish. When do you want to start?'

'In half an hour? I'll get my things together.'

'No tape recorder!'

'No problem. Where shall we do this?'

'In my office. I'll show you.'

They went back down the steep stairs to the hall and on to the lift, which took them down a floor to his office. When he made no move to invite her inside, Eleanor smiled politely, told him she'd return in half an hour and went back up to the guest room.

Alex watched her go, already regretting he'd agreed to this. He shrugged impatiently and reminded himself that Eleanor deserved her reward. But in return for the interview he had given no other journalist he deserved a reward too, of the kind that Ms Markham was supremely equipped to give him. He smiled as he checked the array of technology lining the room, had a brief conversation with Stefan and then placed a chair in front of the desk he'd had shipped from London. He transferred all paperwork to the drawers and sat back behind the desk to wait.

CHAPTER FIVE

ELEANOR took a minute or two to tidy up then packed her bag, which looked very much the worse for wear after its use as a weapon. She went down in the lift to tap on the office door, and when bidden to enter halted on the threshold, deeply impressed.

'What an amazing workplace,' she commented, and smiled at Alex as he stood up. 'I'm a bit early.'

'Can't wait to get to work?' He waved a hand at the chair in front of the desk and seated himself behind it. 'Let's make a start.'

Eleanor pulled the chair close, took the tools of her trade from her bag and looked across at the man enthroned in his massive leather chair. 'May I take a photograph?'

Alex nodded reluctantly. 'But just of me, please, not the room.'

She focused on his face and took two shots, then opened her notebook and sat with pencil poised.

Eleanor had not expected the interview to be easy, but getting Alexei to talk about his achievements was uphill work. There was to be no mention of anything personal, including his family. He was willing to discuss the company he'd founded in his teens because it had given him the means for expansion into the other ventures which had brought him global success. He gave her concise information about most of his interests, but on the subject of his philanthropy he was more guarded. His financial support was given to certain deserving causes only after careful research to make sure the funds went straight to those most in need, rather than into the pockets of administrators.

'May I mention the work here on Kyrkiros?' asked Eleanor.

'Certainly—good PR for the project.'

'What made you take on this particular island?'

'I had good reason to be grateful to the inhabitants.'

'May I ask why?'

Alex was silent for a moment then shrugged as though coming to a decision. 'You can stop there for a minute.'

Eleanor frowned. 'Can't you explain why you're grateful to them?'

He fixed her with a dark, warning eye. 'I can, but only in confidence. Since I brought the subject up, I suppose it's only fair to explain, but solely on the strict understanding that you write about the work being done here and not my personal reasons for developing Kyrkiros.'

She put her pencil down and closed the notebook, then sat back. 'Off the record then.'

Alex was silent for a while as though picking and choosing how much information to give her, then began describing a holiday taken after graduation—a stay in the home of a university friend on Crete.

'Sailing in the Aegean was a great way to de-stress after the hard graft of finals. I spent most of that last fortnight with Ari in the family dinghy,' Alex told her. 'But one day we went farther than usual and when a storm blew up it swept us God knows how far off-course. We both fought hard to keep her afloat but when the dinghy finally capsized the boom caught Ari's head as we went overboard. I managed to hook an arm in Ari's life-jacket and held on for what felt like eternity until we were rescued.' He smiled grimly. 'Poseidon must have been watching over us.'

Eleanor gazed at him in sudden comprehension. 'You were rescued by people here on Kyrkiros?'

'*I* was, yes. I passed out at some point, so I was pretty much out of it for a while. When I finally woke up my broken arm was in a cast, I had the mother of all headaches, every bone in my body was throbbing in sympathy and I was lying on a bed here in the *Kastro*, in what is now the kitchen. I woke with total recall, wild with anxiety about Ari.' Alex smiled grimly. 'Sofia's husband had hauled me into his boat, but Ari had been detached from me by Dion Aristides and taken to his place on nearby Naros.'

'Wouldn't it have been easier to take care of you both in the same place?'

'Dion ordered the others to wait to find out exactly who we were and whether we were married.'

'*Married*?'

Alex smiled. 'My fellow castaway was Arianna Marinos. She was cared for by Dion's female servants, while Sophia and Georg looked after me. Anxious parents soon arrived on the scene, but it was some time before Ari was well enough to travel. Her mother stayed with her at Dion's place and after a visit to check on her I left with my parents. Ari and I both recovered, I got on with my life and eventually attended her wedding on Crete,' he said wryly. 'One look at Dion's handsome face when she finally woke up, and Ari had no eyes for anyone else, including me.'

Wow, thought Eleanor. 'Does she live there with him now?'

'When they're there on the island, yes. Dion does great things with the vineyards there, and after I took over here he agreed to extend his expertise to our Kyrkiros vines. He also oversees those on part of the estate on Crete that Arianna inherited from her father, the place where I'd holidayed with her before she deserted me for another man.' He smiled crookedly. 'It was bad news for this famous hubris of mine. I broke my arm in the process of saving her life, while she broke my heart.'

'It obviously mended,' said Eleanor briskly, secretly sympathetic. 'Was she here for the festival?'

He shook his head. 'Not this year. She's expecting their second child soon, and Dion persuaded her to stay home on Naros.'

Alex's face betrayed no hint of emotion at the mention of children, but something in his tone touched a chord in Eleanor. Or maybe she was attributing sensitivity where he merely felt indifference. 'So what happened next?'

He told her he'd eventually liaised with the newly-wed couple as to the best way to show appreciation for the kindness shown to him by the people of Kyrkiros. At first Dion had been hostile, not only jealous of Alexei Drakos' past relationship with his wife, but suspicious of the young entrepreneur's motives where Kyrkiros was concerned. Alex had made it very clear that his sole aim was to provide steady income for the islanders, show them how to market their produce and thus free them from the financial vagaries that threaten a lifestyle based on fishing. Dion was quick to grasp the advantages of a wider market for the Kyrkiros olives and wine. The grapes grown on the island produced wine with a unique bouquet and flavour, and once marketed with the products of the Aristides and Marinos vineyards the new venture took off at speed after the festival was established as a PR exercise.

Alex had resolved to restore the *Kastro* the first

time he returned to Kyrkiros with his mother to express his thanks to the inhabitants. When he eventually took over the island, Talia expressed her personal gratitude by contributing part of the cost of creating an apartment in the *Kastro* for her son's special retreat, with as much work as possible given to the islanders on restoration of the main building.

'God knows when it will ever be finished,' said Alex. 'But the end result is less important than the security the work gives to the people here. Besides,' he added, 'I quite like the old place the way it is.'

'Whose idea was the bull dance?' asked Eleanor.

'Arianna's. The three of us talked over the best way to attract attention and, Cretan that she is, she suggested putting on some viable version of the bull dance depicted at Knossos. She did the research, devised the dance with a professional choreographer and with his help eventually found a team of dancers acrobatic enough to perform it. Stefan helped with the PR and advertising, and the very first performance was such a success we've never looked back. Though this year's dancers surpassed all the others,' he added. 'You were impressed?'

'An experience I'll never forget,' she assured him. She opened her laptop, pressed a few keys and turned the screen towards him. 'See for yourself.'

Alex studied them then looked up at her with respect. 'These are good—very good. You've captured the antiquity of the scene.' His eyes gleamed as he scrolled to the Minotaur's entrance. 'Zeus! If I didn't know he was flesh and blood I could swear he was the monster he's portraying.' He frowned. 'Theseus is far too pretty, but you were clever to catch him with his axe poised for the kill.' He pushed the laptop back to her. 'So, Eleanor Markham, do you have enough information for this article you've worked so hard to achieve?'

'I think so.' She gathered her belongings together. 'I'll go back to my room now and work on it. I'll give you the draft as soon as it's ready.'

'I thought you wanted to laze in the sun for a while.'

'Work before pleasure,' she said absently, her mind already busy. 'Where will you be when I finish?'

'Here probably, or I might go down and lift some weights for a while.' He took a mobile phone from a drawer and handed it over as he saw her to the door. 'I should have given you this before.'

'I sent emails to my parents instead, but I'm glad of the phone.' She smiled politely. 'Thank you.'

'My number's keyed in on it. If I'm not here, just ring me when you want me. Or I'll ring when I want *you*.'

Something in his tone sent the now-familiar streak of heat through Eleanor as she hurried back to her room, deeply conscious that he was watching her all the way. Shorts had been a risky choice. On the other hand her legs were good. Her *derrière* wasn't bad, either and she was female—and human—enough to be glad of it in the circumstances. She closed the bedroom door behind her and settled down to concentrate on the task in hand as she plugged in her laptop to type up her notes. With only the official facts Alexei Drakos had given her, it would be no easy task to deliver the earth-shaking interview Ross McLean was salivating for, but at least she could describe this beautiful island and give a plug to the work going on here. To add colour she could weave in a little about the owner's aspirations. She sighed. If she could write about the sailing accident and Alex's personal reasons for taking over Kyrkiros, she'd have Ross dancing on his desk.

When she'd finished Eleanor worked up her notes into a first draft. She broke off for a tidying up session in the bathroom and then went back to the laptop. It was just a draft, she reminded herself irritably as she edited it. At last she saved her work, unplugged the laptop and took it down to the office. She knocked and put her head round the door, but the room was empty. She ground her teeth. Now she'd stiffened her resolve enough to let him read the damned article, the man was missing. She left the laptop on the desk and turned to run smack into a hard male body.

Alex seized her by the waist to steady her. 'Careful! Where are you going?'

'To look for you.' The contact sent Eleanor's pulse so high into overdrive she said the first thing that came into her head as she saw his hair. 'You've been swimming again?'

He shook his head as he let her go. 'I've been working out and had a shower afterwards. I made one of the ground floor rooms into a gym. You're welcome to use it.'

She shook her head, smiling ruefully as she backed away. 'Not really my thing, thank you. I just do a bit of Pilates now and then to keep in shape.'

The dark eyes moved over her in a slow head-to-toe scrutiny as she sat down at the desk. 'It works!'

Eleanor firmly ignored the sizzle of heat his comment sent streaking through her and booted up the laptop. She scrolled to the draft of the article and pushed the machine across the desk to him. 'I kept to the letter of the law with your restrictions so it won't take long to read.'

He raised an eyebrow. 'Do I detect a note of censure, Eleanor? What additions would you make to it if I gave you free rein?'

'Personally, I would put in the human interest of how you were rescued by the people of Kyrkiros and that your investment in their welfare is your way of thanking them.'

Alex shook his head with finality. 'That would mean involving others who value their privacy.'

He drew the laptop nearer. 'While I read it, go up and sit in the sun in the roof garden.'

'I'd rather read in my room for a while. I'll take to the roof as a reward after the article's gone.' She gave him Ross McLean's email address. 'If you approve, contact my editor and read the riot act to him before I send it off.'

But back in her room there was no way she could concentrate on someone else's written word. She sat at the window to look down on a view of boats, and a hot sun-baked beach edging ultra-marine sea, feeling like a character in some novel herself, maybe in a fairy tale, looking down from her tower on the world below. Except that she was no princess, and the handsome prince was right here in the tower, probably cutting her article to ribbons as he read it.

When the expected knock came Eleanor braced herself as she opened the door.

Alex smiled. 'It's good. I've made a few minor adjustments, so come back to the office and sort out the final draft. Then send it off and you can relax in the sun at last.'

'Thank you,' she said, relieved. 'Did you contact Ross?'

'I did, and laid down the law about my requirements. His immediate reply gave assurances that no syllable would be changed.'

'I wish I'd been there to see his face when he got the email!'

'You could have waited to give him the piece until you got back.'

She shook her head. 'Better this way.'

'But you won't be there to see the article in print.'

Eleanor grinned. 'Knowing Ross, he'll have it framed on his office wall of fame by the time I get back.'

Alex held out the chair in front of his desk for her, and pushed the laptop over, along with a page of notes. 'These are my revisions. Shall I leave you to it?'

She cast her eyes over the list. 'It won't take long.'

He leaned back in his chair. 'Then I'll stay.'

She nodded absently and set to work.

Alexei watched the intent, sun-bronzed face with pleasure which reinforced his plan of the night before. Strands of glossy dark hair had escaped their moorings to lie against Eleanor's cheeks, but she seemed unaware of them, or of him or anything else, as she incorporated his alterations into her text. She finished very quickly, but then sat, teeth caught in her bottom lip as she read through the article twice before she was satisfied.

He felt a surprising pang of something very like tenderness at her total absorption. Eleanor Markham was no beauty, but there was something about her narrow, intelligent face that appealed to him as much as—even far more than—the glossy, highly finished ones he mixed with socially here in Athens and London, also in New York from time to time. He was certain that nature alone was responsible for the curves outlined by her shirt and, though she had worn make-up the night before, there was none in evidence today. He might dislike her profession, but he liked Eleanor.

He must like her a lot, he thought sardonically. It was not a habit of his to discuss his personal life with anyone, not even his mother, yet he'd found himself actually describing his schooldays to Eleanor. Even more unusually, he had complete confidence in her assurance that what he required kept off the record would stay that way. His mother had been right—as always. The company of an intelligent woman was a refreshing change, and he was by no means ready to part with this one just yet.

'There,' she said at last and slid the laptop over to him. 'If you're satisfied I'll get it off to Ross.'

After which, of course, she would want to take off immediately for Crete to catch a plane home. As Alex read the revised draft his brain, long accustomed to dealing with several things at once, began devising ways to keep her here longer—not only to take her to bed but because he enjoyed her company. Persuading a woman to stay with him was new. From the time he'd reached his present stature in his early teens, women had been there for the taking, from the neighbours' daughters he met in Corfu to the women encountered in college and in the business world afterwards. But, with his parents' union as example, marriage held no appeal. His normal male appetites were catered for by sophisticated beauties who appealed to his senses only, never to his heart. Loving someone madly, as both his parents had done, was a fate he had taken pains to avoid. Not, he realised, frowning, that he had any knowledge of pain in a romantic relationship. Arianna might have dented his pride a little, but his heart had survived undamaged.

'Is it that bad?' demanded Eleanor. 'Shall I do more work on it?'

Alex shook his head. 'No. It's fine as it is. I always frown when I concentrate.'

'You don't object to the touches I put in?'

'No. They make me sound human, so leave them. You write well.' He pushed the laptop back to her. 'All yours; make your editor happy.'

Eleanor was only too glad to speed the article on its way, along with the photograph which really pleased her. It portrayed Alexei Drakos in exactly the right light, his air of power unmistakeable.

'Just wait for McLean to acknowledge it,' said Alex. 'Then afterwards you can relax and enjoy some lunch before you go up to the roof to sunbathe.'

'An attractive programme,' she agreed, and smiled wryly as the expected email popped into her inbox. 'Here it is.'

Alex came round the desk to look over her shoulder.

'"Good girl! Many thanks, RMcL."'

'Good girl!' said Eleanor in disgust, and shut the laptop.

'You prefer "woman"?' said Alex, amused.

'Would you like it if someone said "good boy"?'

'Point taken. Let me soothe your indignation with a glass of vintage Kyrkiros wine.'

Eleanor agreed gratefully. She felt utterly wrung out, which was ridiculous. Spending the morning on one solitary article wouldn't normally be exhausting, but getting one so important so absolutely right, and with Alexei looking on as she worked, had been a draining experience. To sink into a comfortable sofa and look out at the view as she drank her celebratory wine was a treat she deserved after the effort taken to get the interview. Though she had Talia to thank for that, she knew only too well.

'I need a wash before lunch,' she told Alex. 'I won't be long.'

'Take your time.' He smiled. Something he was doing a lot more lately since he'd met Eleanor Markham. 'But not too much. You need sustenance after all your hard work.'

'Fifteen minutes,' Eleanor promised, and hurried off to her room. Since she was finally going to enjoy her time in the sun later, she put on the relatively conservative swimwear she wore when travelling alone, covered it with a loose pink shirt and white jeans and thrust her feet into pink flip-flops. She slapped on some moisturiser and lip gloss, brushed out her hair and put sun block, book and dark glasses in the tote bag.

'You're on time,' said Alex as she joined him in the tower room. 'A pearl among women. You notice I said *women*?'

She laughed, feeling suddenly euphoric now she'd achieved the impossible and not only written, but actually sent off, her exclusive about Alexei Drakos. 'Duly noted,' she assured him and accepted the brimming glass he handed her. 'Thank you. I really need this.'

'I asked for a salad with some of Sofia's bread for ballast,' said Alex, indicating the meal set out on the table. 'We can eat something more substantial for dinner.'

Eleanor felt a little bubble of excitement rise somewhere inside at the prospect, and sternly reminded herself that their evening together was a matter of obligation for Alexei Drakos, not a dinner date. 'Right now a cold meal is exactly what

I need.' She raised her glass in toast. 'Plus this, of course. You make seriously good wine here on Kirkyros.'

'Dion is a notable winemaker and a hard task-master on the subject of quality. I just make sure the wine sells. And drink it,' he added as he touched his glass to hers.

Eleanor took another sip and rolled it round her tongue. 'It has a flavour all its own—something like a rosé, but with more body. And,' she added, smiling at him, 'Delicious though it is, I'll stick to one glass. It's heady stuff.'

Between them they polished off most of the savoury bread with the entire platter of crayfish salad, talking so easily together, for a change, during the meal that Eleanor almost accepted when Alex offered more wine, but then shook her head and filled a glass from a jug of ice water instead.

'Prudent lady,' he observed lazily.

'I've been looking forward to my session in the sun too much to risk a headache!' She got up. 'Talking of which, if you'll excuse me I'll now make my way to your roof garden at last.'

Alex offered to accompany her, but Eleanor smiled at him politely and shook her head.

'I'm sure you have things to do, so I'll leave you in peace. Tell Sofia the lunch was fabulous.'

'It was.' Alex opened the door for her. 'But for me that had more to do with the charming company than the food.' He touched her hair fleetingly and smiled into her eyes. 'It would be wise to wear a hat.'

She nodded jerkily. 'I'll pop into my room and collect one on the way.'

Alex leaned in the doorway, watching her as she rushed along the hall at such speed she lost one of her flip-flops and had to bend to snatch it up. He smiled. Eleanor was very wary of him, which was all to the good. Her lack of coquetry was so appealing, he would take great pleasure in coaxing her into his bed. But instead of following her, as instinct urged, he turned away to his office to ring Stefan. He would give Eleanor her half hour in the sun before he joined her to make sure all was well with his guest, as any host worth his salt would do. After a report from Stefan, he gave his assistant a few comprehensive instructions then went back to the window to look down at the beach below, feeling restless again after the business discussion. The part of him that detested idleness was urging him to get back to take the reins in Athens, or to London to do the same there. But the part of him he usually kept in firm control was happy to stay here lotus-eating for a while.

A pity he couldn't take Eleanor on a tour of the island rather than keeping her locked up with him in the *Kastro*, but it was better to take no chances until he saw her off on her flight from Crete. His hands clenched. He would never forget the horror of hearing his mother scream his name as she was snatched almost from under his nose, nor the harsh censure he'd received from his father for not taking more care of her—which had stung all the more for being deserved. He would make damned sure nothing happened to Eleanor Markham.

At the thought of his mother Alex felt a sudden urge to make sure all was well with her, and rang to tell her he'd done her bidding like a good son and Eleanor's article had been sent off to her editor. Talia was delighted. She praised him lavishly and advised him to make the most of the time he was spending with his guest.

'You are right to keep her safe there with you, Alexei *mou*,' she said lovingly. 'Give Eleanor my good wishes and make her promise to visit me when she gets home.'

CHAPTER SIX

ELEANOR lay perfectly still on one of the long chairs in the roof garden, her face in the shade under the parasol, and the rest of her—liberally coated with sun block—stretched out in the sun to top up her tan. For once she had no desire to read. Her mind was occupied with Alexei, and the abundance of physical attributes bestowed on him by nature. The few natural blondes of her acquaintance would kill to possess curling lashes like his; she shook her head in sudden impatience. It was time to leave this magical place. If she stayed any longer she'd risk falling for the man, which would be the height of stupidity from so many points of view she should put it out of her mind—and less cerebral parts—right now. After their hostile start he'd now warmed towards her to a very gratifying degree, it was true; enough to talk on subjects she was pretty sure he never discussed with anyone other than his mother. And on the subject of

Arianna, maybe not even to Talia. But anything hotter than that was out of the question, as she well knew.

She smiled bleakly. The only man in her past she had ever felt actual lust for had made it clear he looked on her as the perfect friend. Sexy bedmates were two a penny, he'd told her, but an intelligent female friend like Eleanor Markham was a pearl beyond price. Alex had brought up the pearl thing, too. She was tired of it.

Alex opened the door onto the roof garden quietly, and stood very still at the sight of Eleanor lying in the sun in a relatively modest bikini. Strangely, it made her far more desirable than the flaunted assets of most holiday makers, even with a dark bruise visible on her ribcage. Hands clenched at the thought of the man who had caused it, and he stood looking at her so long she stirred.

'I disturbed you,' he said quietly, joining her.

Eleanor sat up and pulled her shirt on. 'I've had enough sun for now anyway.' She smiled at him brightly. 'This is a perfect place to sunbathe. Do you spend a lot of time up here?'

'Very little.' He sat down beside her, close

enough to breathe in the scent of warm, sun-kissed female, and had to clench his hands to keep from touching the glowing skin. 'It was the general idea when I had the work done up here but I rarely have the time.'

She shook her head in mock-disapproval. 'Your empire would hardly disintegrate if you took half an hour off now and then, surely?'

He smiled wryly. 'You sound just like my mother—who, by the way, asked me to pass on her good wishes when I spoke to her earlier.'

Eleanor's eyes softened behind her dark lenses. 'How sweet of her. Does she come up here to sun-bathe?'

Alex gave a snort of laughter. 'Never! She keeps that complexion of hers well protected from the sun. Christo, the photographer who made her famous, laid the law down from the start.'

Eleanor nodded. 'I bought my mother the book of portraits he published, solely because the majority of them were of Talia Kazan. He described her in his foreword as his Greek goddess muse.'

'He was furious when she gave up her career to marry my father.' Alex smiled sardonically. 'Christo is a Londoner from the East End, real name Chris Higgins, who discovered her when she was a schoolgirl on holiday in London. The camera loved her and because she was in love with London, and excited by the idea of independence, she persuaded her father to let her work with the celebrated Christo. My grandfather could never deny her anything, so Talia Kazan stayed in London and became famous almost overnight. Her face was on the cover of every glossy magazine at one time or another.'

Eleanor nodded. 'My mother still has some of them. She always wondered why Talia Kazan's career ended so abruptly.'

'Christo blamed my father for his muse's desertion, but in actual fact the novelty of a modelling career wore off for her very quickly. The ex-policewoman my grandfather hired as Talia's companion and minder was leaving her to get married, and if it hadn't been for Christo and his pleas my mother would have given it up long before she met Milo Drakos. She was involved in a fashion shoot in winter near the Greek embassy in London. It was a bitterly cold day and my father came out of the building to see her shivering in a flimsy summer dress. He stripped off his coat, wrapped her in it and, ignoring Christo's violent objections, swept her into a taxi with her minder and took her home.'

'How romantic!' Eleanor smiled at him. 'It was love at first sight?'

His mouth twisted. 'If it was, it didn't last long.' He turned away as Yannis appeared, carefully carrying a tray. 'I thought you might be thirsty.'

'How kind of you.' Eleanor smiled at the boy. '*Efcharisto,* Yannis.'

Alex filled two glasses with fruit juice and ice and handed one to Eleanor. 'I trust you're taking note.'

'That you're waiting on me? I'm honoured.'

'As you should be.' He touched his glass to hers, giving her that calculated look again.

'You mean the women you know are perfectly happy to wait on you all the time?'

'If they're not, they've never said so.'

Of course they hadn't!

He chuckled. 'You have a very expressive face, *kyria* journalist. Those cat's eyes of yours shoot off sparks of disapproval.'

'*Cat's* eyes!' she retorted. 'Thanks a lot.'

'I mean that they are gold in some light, like a lioness,' Alex said, surprising her.

'Hazel,' said Eleanor, and downed some of her drink. 'That's what it says on my passport,' she added as he looked blank.

'Hazel,' he repeated. 'I'll remember that.'

Eleanor gave him a sidelong, suspicious look. If he never came up here normally, why was he here now?

'What is it?' he asked.

She put her sunglasses back on. 'Would you be kind enough to take me over to Karpyros tomorrow to get the ferry to Crete, please?'

Alex frowned. 'You're so desperate to get away?'

Not nearly as much as she should be. 'I'm very conscious that I'm keeping you here when you should be wherever you're due next, so—'

'So now the article has gone off, you're unwilling to stay a second longer than necessary.'

'That's not what I meant. I'm just trying to be as little trouble to you as possible.'

He reached out and whipped the sunglasses from her face. 'I dislike staring into blank lenses. The earliest flight I could arrange is in two days' time. So you must endure your captivity until then.'

'I'm sorry to be such a nuisance for you.' Eleanor found it hard not to fidget under the black, relentless gaze. 'But you don't have to stay with me. I'm safe enough here with Sofia and Yannis and your security people. Just organise someone to get me over to Karpyros to catch the ferry on the day and you can be on your way first thing tomorrow. Or even tonight.'

His smile set her alarm bells ringing. 'You are unflatteringly anxious to get rid of me, while I am only too delighted to spend extra time in *your* company.' His eyes hardened. 'I will not let you out of my sight until I see you safely on that plane, Eleanor Markham.'

She stared at him in surprise. 'Why? It's not so long since you threatened to have me fired from my job.'

'I admit that in my concern for my mother—and my aversion to the media—I was too quick to accuse. But I have atoned for that. If nothing else, you can add a unique qualification to your CV should you seek another job—the only journalist to achieve an interview with Alexei Drakos.'

Eleanor grinned. 'There goes that hubris again.'

He shrugged his formidable shoulders. 'If you mean I am proud of what I have achieved in my life, I admit that. But is it so strange that I prefer to keep my personal life private?'

'Not in the least. Yet you talked to me about some of it. Why?'

'I wish I knew. And wish now I had not.' The compelling eyes locked on hers again. 'Do not betray my confidence, Eleanor Markham.'

'I won't, ever,' she assured him.

'Even though you could be paid big money for some of the information I gave you?'

'Only if I sold it to another paper. And, since I like the job I have now, I won't do that. Besides,' she added. 'I gave you my word.'

'So you did.' Alex handed the sunglasses over. 'Tell me about your life in England. You have a house there?'

'I share one with a college friend. Originally there were four of us, but due to career changes the other two left, so now I live upstairs and the ground floor is Pat's territory.' She smiled. 'It works well because I'm away so much.'

'Who owns the house?'

'The landlord. We rent.'

Alex looked at her curiously. 'Wouldn't it be better to buy a house?'

'Of course. But only when I can afford to live alone in one.'

'You have no wish to marry?'

She smiled wryly. 'I'm all too familiar with the stress of sharing a house. I'd have to think long and hard before sharing my entire life with a man.'

He nodded. 'I understand that. When I see the life Arianna has made with Dion, I have no envy, even though I once cared for her.'

'You said she broke your heart!'

'I was dramatic to win your sympathy,' he said shamelessly and grinned. 'Did I succeed?'

'Fleetingly.' She hesitated. 'Don't you want children?'

He shrugged. 'I would like a son one day, but marriage is unnecessary for that.'

Her eyes flashed. 'You mean you would just select an appropriate mother for your son? What then? Would he just spend his summer holidays with you?'

'*Ochi*! He would live with me permanently.'

'How about the mother?'

'She could stay also, if she wished.'

'Big of you! But if she's the normal breed of mother you won't separate her from her son with a crowbar.' She smiled. 'Not that I need tell you that.'

'True,' he conceded. 'My mother found it hard to part with me for just the brief times I spent time with my father. Even so, she kept rigidly to the terms of their agreement until I was eighteen, at which point the delightful Melania came into his life. I spent only one holiday in Corfu with them and never went back.' He smiled sardonically. 'No one enjoyed that holiday—my father, his mistress and I least of all. I became ill soon after I arrived, and left after only a few days. That was my last holiday with my father.'

'It must have been hard for your mother to bring you up alone.' Eleanor's sympathy for Talia was growing by the minute.

'Until I went to England to school my grandfather was always there to help her when I got out of hand, as boys do. My grandmother died when I was young, and I hardly remember her, but Cyrus was a big part of my life. He adored my mother. It must have been hard for him to let her work with

Christo.' He shook his head suddenly. 'Amazing! I find myself telling you things I never speak of to anyone else, Eleanor Markham.'

She smiled. 'Probably because I have infinite experience in providing a listening ear—right through school, college and afterwards when I shared a house with friends. When they had man trouble—a pretty regular occurrence—I provided tea and sympathy and even mopping up.'

'Did they return the favour?' he said, amused.

She shook her head. 'I kept my woes to myself.'

'As I said before, a pearl among women!'

The pearl thing again! 'You've forgotten my temper.'

Alex laughed. 'I assure you I have not. Those eyes of yours flash like warning lights when you are angry. I admire such passion in a woman.'

She tried to keep her expression neutral. No one had ever said anything like that to her before. 'Contrary to your belief, *kyrie* Drakos, I hardly ever lose my temper.'

'Beating men up is not a habit for you?'

'No.' She chuckled. 'So rest easy, you're in no danger from me.'

'A great relief,' he said with sarcasm, then

frowned as a sudden gust of wind rattled the screen. He got up to look out from the balustrade. 'Eleanor, we must go down. A storm is coming. You can read in the tower room instead.'

She pulled on her jeans hurriedly. 'I can read in my room.'

'Then I will feel like your jailer. I shall work in my office. You can have the tower room to yourself and watch the storm coming.'

Not a prospect Eleanor fancied at all. But she fancied solitude in her room even less. 'Thank you. I'll run my laptop on the battery and do some work.'

A gust of wind caught her as she made for the door. Alex shot out an arm to steady her, took charge of her bag and thrust her through the doorway as the wind began to rise in earnest. He slammed the door closed behind them and followed her down to her room.

'You are quite safe here, Eleanor. If the electricity fails we have an emergency generator.'

'Good to know.' She smiled brightly.

'I will see you later.' He handed her bag over and strode rapidly along the hall rather than surrender to the urge to stay with her and forget about work for once.

Eleanor closed the door as the wind rose to new heights. She crossed to the windows to see people rushing to haul boats up the beach out of danger and shivered enough to decide on a hot shower. She had just finished dressing when Sofia came to tell her tea was waiting in the tower room.

'*Efcharisto,* Sofia.'

The woman nodded in approval at Eleanor's heavy cotton sweater. 'Good. It will be colder soon.'

Eleanor grabbed her laptop and hurried along to the brightly lit tower room to check the storm's progress from the windows but found the view obscured by spray. She ate one of Sofia's pastries and settled back with her tea as the wind mounted in increasing fury. Thankful she'd been spared weather like this during her island-hopping, she got down to some serious editing on the first of her travel articles. She worked steadily in an effort to ignore the escalating storm until lightning sizzled through the room accompanied by a deafening crack of thunder, and the lights went out.

Alex raced in, training one of the torches he held on her face. 'Eleanor—are you all right?'

'Just startled,' she assured him breathlessly, hoping he hadn't heard her screech of fright.

He laughed. 'I almost said good girl, but remembered you don't like that.'

Eleanor grinned. 'Anyway—' She was just about to assure him she was perfectly fine when more flashes and bangs cut her off. 'Wow,' she said shakily when she could be heard. 'The storms are mega-noisy in these parts.'

'But you are safe here, Eleanor. I regret that I must leave you to go down to check on Sofia and give Theo a hand with the generator. I can't use the lift, obviously, but I'll be as quick as I can. Will you be all right alone?'

'Of course.' What else could she say?

'I'll leave you a torch.'

'Thank you.' Eleanor winced as the room was lit up by lightning, but this time the thunder was less immediate. 'There,' she said brightly. 'Farther away already.'

Alex laughed and startled her by bending to plant a kiss on her mouth. 'I'll be back as soon as I can.'

Eleanor listened to his footsteps as he raced along the hall to the stairs, then took in a deep breath and returned to her work. But the storm made concentration impossible. Alex's kiss hadn't helped, either. Those lips of his tasted as good as they looked. She closed the laptop and went back to the sofa with the torch alight on the table beside her, passing the time by counting the seconds between each flash and crack of thunder. She surprised herself by actually chuckling when some of the cracks and flashes still came together. Her childhood method didn't apply to Greek storms; Poseidon ruled in these parts.

The lights finally came on after a wait so long the storm had retreated to other parts of the Aegean and stars were blazing in a clear sky. Eleanor turned from the windows in relief when she heard someone in the hall and ran to the door with a smile, which faded abruptly when she saw no sign of Alex. Nor of anyone else. She spun round to collect her laptop and flew along the hall, the creaks and groans of the ancient building rocketing her in a headlong rush to her room. She locked the door behind her and switched on the light, laughing at herself when she had her breath back.

Who was she keeping out, for heaven's sake? It took a few deep, even breaths before she calmed down, only to jump yards as the phone Alex had given her rang in her bag.

'Hello?' she said breathlessly.

'Sorry to be so long, Eleanor, are you all right?'

'Now the storm's moved away, yes.'

'Good. I'm just finishing up here. Sofia says dinner will be ready in half an hour or so, which gives me time to clean up.'

The news that Alex was on his way was hugely welcome. Eleanor frowned. But if he was still down below, whose footsteps had she heard? This might be a very modern apartment, but alone up here she was very conscious of the antiquity of the rest of the building. It would hardly be surprising if there were ghosts. Hoping any in residence were the benevolent kind, she tidied up, collected her book and left her room as Alex emerged from the lift.

'I'm filthy,' he told her, grinning like a schoolboy. 'Sofia wanted me to wash in her kitchen, but I need to stand under a very hot shower. Will you wait for me in the tower room?'

'Of course, take your time. Something wrong with the generator?'

He nodded. 'But we put it right—eventually.'

Eleanor went back to the tower room, feeling a lot happier, even able to laugh at herself for scurrying along the hall earlier like a scared rabbit. Not something she would share with Alex. She doubted he was scared of anything. She crossed the beautiful, uncluttered room to look out at the view of moonlight reflected on the now flat calm of the sea. It was easy to picture Jason, back in the mists of time, passing by out there in the *Argo* on his quest for the golden fleece. She stiffened at the sound of footsteps, but this time it was the solidly real Sofia arriving with a tray of olives and nuts.

'Are you well, *kyria*?' she asked anxiously. 'I was worried for you alone up here in the storm, but I cannot manage the old steps in the dark. I thank the good God—and *kyrie* Alexei—for the blessing of the lift.'

Having understood about half of that, Eleanor nodded, smiling. 'I'm fine.' It was true enough now that the lights were on and Alex was close at hand.

'Dinner very soon,' Sofia promised, and went

hurrying off to exchange a word with Alex in the hall.

Eleanor made no attempt to hide how glad she was to see him. His thin shirt clung to him as if he'd put it on while his skin was damp, revealing musculature so impressive she was seized with an overwhelming desire to run her hands over his chest and whipped them behind her back to avoid temptation.

'Sorry to be so long,' Alex smiled with sympathy. 'It must have been quite an ordeal up here on your own in the storm. Did you work to pass the time?'

'I tried but I couldn't concentrate so I reverted to counting the seconds between the lightning strikes instead.'

'Then you must need a drink as much as I do.' He filled two glasses and handed one to her.

Eleanor settled down in a corner of the sofa with a sigh of pleasure. 'Is power failure a regular occurrence here?'

'Yes.' He joined her and touched his glass to hers. 'But tonight there was a problem with the generator.' He grinned. 'I rather enjoy the challenge of mastering the thing.'

She laughed. 'You mean you were having fun down there?'

'Not this time. I was concerned about you up here on your own.'

'It's a bit daunting in the dark,' Eleanor admitted, and smiled as Sofia came in with a dish of savouries. 'No Yannis tonight?'

'His friend Markos is spending the night with him,' said his mother, looking anxious. 'They were out in the rain to secure boats and needed a hot bath.' She put a platter of small savoury pies on the table in front of them. 'Eat now while they are warm; I will be back soon with your dinner.'

Alex smiled at her affectionately. '*Efcharisto,* Sofia. Did the power cut affect the meal?'

'No, *kyrie*, it is slow-cooked lamb and kept its heat,' she assured him as she hurried out.

'Thank God for that,' said Alex devoutly and pushed the platter of pastries towards Eleanor. 'These are my mother's favourites, so you're honoured. Sofia rarely makes them for anyone else, except for the festival, where they sell like—'

'Hot cakes?' Eleanor grinned and sampled one, enjoying the taste of cheese and herbs so much she finished it before saying a word. 'Wow. You'd better make a start or I might eat the lot.'

He looked amused. 'Instead you shall share the rest with me before any more accidents prevent us.'

'If the lights go again, I'll come with you to help.' Eleanor's eyes sparkled as they sat down together. 'I'm pretty handy with a screw driver.'

'Then I should have taken you with me tonight.' He toasted her with his glass. 'To a lady of many talents.'

She shook her head. 'Not really. I pride myself on being good at my job, and I can cook a bit, but I can't sing or play a musical instrument.'

'But you have a talent for friendship.'

Eleanor sighed. 'I shouldn't have boasted to you about that.'

'You had no need. I know just how good a friend you can be.'

She turned on him. 'How, exactly?'

'Because you flew to my mother's aid without a thought for your own safety.' He frowned. 'Your eyes are giving off angry sparks again. You dislike the label of good friend?'

'By some people, no.'

'But others you object to?'

'Just one, really—a man who once told me beddable women were two a penny, but I was that rarity, a woman he valued as the perfect friend.' Eleanor turned away. 'Not what I wanted to hear. I'd fondly imagined he wanted me as a lover.'

'He was the stupid one if he did not.' Alex turned her face to his. 'You are a very desirable woman, Eleanor Markham.'

'Thank you.'

'It's the simple truth,' he assured her.

Face hot, Eleanor changed the subject. 'I hope Yannis won't have caught cold.'

'He won't care as long as he secured his boat— which is the love of his life. He takes it over to Karpyros with Markos at weekends to hang out with friends there.'

'You bought it for him?'

'I bought it for his use, yes. My own is powered by a bigger engine. Yannis is forbidden to go near it.'

'By you?'

'By his mother. His father drowned in a storm while fishing, so it took much persuasion for her to let Yannis out in a boat at all at first. But, because life without one is difficult here, she eventually gave in.' Alex eyed the empty plate in rueful surprise. 'I've devoured the lot. My apologies, Eleanor.'

'None needed. Dinner's on its way.'

'So it is. You have very sharp ears!'

'Not always a blessing. I sometimes hear things I'd rather not.' Or weren't even real, like phantom footsteps in the hall. She got up as Sofia trundled the trolley into the room, and with a smile began transferring dishes of vegetables to the table while Sofia removed parchment from a joint of meat to release a mouth-watering aroma into the room.

'Lamb,' Sofia informed her. 'You like it?'

Thankful it wasn't goat, Eleanor nodded fervently. 'I love it.'

'I will be back later to clear. Eat well.'

Alex got to work with a carving knife while Eleanor served the vegetables, and silence reigned for a while as they fell on the food with hunger fuelled by hard labour on Alex's part and post-storm euphoria on his guest's.

'This is just wonderful,' she told him after a while.

He nodded. 'Sofia is a skilled cook. We were

lucky she prepared a dish which survived the power cut.'

'Very lucky!' She hesitated. 'Is there any news about who hired Spiro Baris?'

'No, but my people are working on it,' Alex said grimly. 'When I find out I will report to my father, as he demanded. And then the man responsible will curse the day he thought of kidnapping my mother.' His laugh was short and mirthless. 'Because my parents are divorced, the idiot was unaware he risked Milo Drakos' revenge as well as mine.'

'Would an enormous ransom have been demanded?'

'Probably. I would have given all I possess to get my mother back. And, to be fair, so would my father.' Alex smiled. 'But due to your bravery, Eleanor, my mother and my bank balance survived unharmed—and so, thank God, did you. I owe you more than I can ever repay.'

She shook her head. 'The interview was reward enough.'

'Yet it benefited your editor more than you.'

'But it gave me enormous satisfaction. I don't believe Ross McLean thought for a moment that

I would actually persuade you to talk to me.' Eleanor's eyes sparkled. 'It's a personal triumph to prove him wrong.'

'You don't like him?'

'Actually, I do. He's very good at his job, and I've learned a lot from him. Ross just has this thing about college graduates because he's had to rely on experience and hard graft to achieve his success in the profession, and never tires of saying so.' She got to her feet. 'Sofia's on her way so I'll just stack these things in the trolley, ready for her.'

'You really do have extraordinary hearing,' said Alex, amused when Sofia arrived as Eleanor put the last of the plates away.

'How is Yannis, Sofia?' she asked.

The woman looked anxious. 'Very hot, and he is coughing, but he won't let me send Markos home.' She shrugged. 'It is company for him.'

Alex smiled in reassurance. 'In the morning, if he's not better I'll get him to a doctor.'

Eleanor searched through her bag for some painkillers and handed them to Sofia. 'Would this help?'

Alex eyed her with respect as he translated the

instructions on the medication for Sofia, who responded with a flood of gratitude for the *kyria* and went hurrying off with the trolley.

'It was just four pills, enough for tonight and in the morning,' said Eleanor. 'So he won't come to any harm.'

'How did we all survive on Kyrkiros before you arrived?' said Alex, and took her by the shoulders, shaking her slightly when her eyes flashed fire at him. 'I was joking. I'm sincerely grateful to you, Eleanor.'

'I don't need your gratitude,' she retorted, trying to get free, but he held her fast, his eyes filled with sudden heat.

'So what *do* you need?' His hands tightened. 'You've had the interview as your reward. Now, *kyria* journalist, I'll take mine.' He bent his head and kissed her, then kissed her again with heat that made her head reel, the meeting of tongue with tongue a match applied to kindling. He pulled her up on her toes, shaping every inch of her against his aroused body as his mouth seduced hers into such helpless response they were both breathing like long-distance runners when he raised his head at last. Very slowly he slackened his hold until she was standing square on her feet again, but he held her fast when she tried to move away. 'Are you so desperate to get away from me?' he demanded hoarsely.

Since it was obvious that her body was deliriously happy where it was, she didn't bother to lie. 'No,' she blurted. 'But I should be.'

'Why? Because my body is telling you I want to be your lover?'

Eleanor heaved in as deep a breath as she could; held so close to his chest. 'You mean you want to sleep with me tonight?' she demanded.

'Not sleep.' The note in his voice made her knees tremble. 'I want to make love to you—and not just tonight but every moment possible before you leave.'

And there it was. She sighed as the adrenaline drained away. 'This may sound coy and unbelievable to you,' she said into his chest, 'But the word "leave" is the clincher. I don't do holiday romances.'

He tipped her face up, his dark eyes locked on hers for an instant; then the heavy lids came down like shutters as he let her go to put space between them. 'But you do much damage to this famous hubris of mine, Eleanor Markham.' He shrugged, suddenly nonchalant. 'Ah well, if you won't sleep with me let us have coffee and go off to our separate beds.'

His about-turn was so deflating Eleanor had to force a smile. 'I'll pass on the coffee, thanks. Sofia's brought some mineral water. I'll take that with me instead.' She paused on her way to the door to look up into the sculpted, handsome face, now blank as a mask bar the nerve throbbing at the corner of the mouth that had just kissed her into a response new in her life. 'Goodnight. And, by the way, thank you.'

'For wanting you for a lover, not a friend?' he said, so quick on the uptake she smiled ruefully.

'Exactly.'

'Honest lady.' His eyes darkened. 'Now go. Take your scruples off to bed.'

Eleanor smiled sweetly and marched off down the hall at speed, fuelled by disappointment when he made no move to follow her.

CHAPTER SEVEN

DUE to a new fondness for the miracle of electricity, Eleanor left the bedside lamp on for company when she was ready for bed, but sleep was hard to come by. She tossed and turned for what seemed like hours, prey to unfamiliar sexual frustration. She finally drifted into an uneasy, restless doze, but woke suddenly, heart pounding. She sat bolt-upright, cold sweat breaking out over her forehead as she stared in horror at the nightmare apparition in the open doorway. She uttered a hoarse scream and scrambled out of bed, so awkward in her terror she tripped and fell and for the first time in her life fainted dead away.

Eleanor came round pressed against Alex's bare chest, his heart thumping like a drum against her cheek.

'You're safe, *agapi mou*,' he assured her, breathing hard. 'You had a bad dream.'

She opened her eyes a crack, afraid of what she

might see, but there was no monstrous, terrifying figure in the open doorway. She heaved in a deep, unsteady breath. 'It was just a nightmare?'

'A very bad one, by your scream.' He rubbed his cheek against her hair, his arms tightening protectively. 'It took years off my life.'

'Off mine too. It was so real. He was standing in the doorway with those great crystal eyes staring at me.' She swallowed convulsively.

Alex tipped her face up to his. 'Crystal eyes?'

Eleanor nodded. 'Like the dancer. A bull's head on a human male body.'

He smiled indulgently. 'A nightmare indeed!'

'Sorry to involve you in it—why are we sitting on the floor?'

'I found you there. I broke the Olympic sprint record to get here when you screamed, and found you unconscious on the floor.' He got to his feet, picked her up and put her back against the pillows. 'You gave me such a scare. Are you better now?'

She shook her head. 'Not really.'

'I'll go down to the kitchen and look for my mother's tea.'

'*No*! Please. Don't leave me alone up here.' She

tried to smile. 'Sorry to be such a coward, but the monster in the doorway seemed horribly real.'

Alex sat on the edge of the bed, eyes narrowed. 'You left your door open?'

Eleanor frowned as she raked her hair back from her perspiring forehead. 'Of course not. I was hardly likely to get ready for bed with it wide open.'

'Not after the conversation we'd just had,' he agreed dryly. 'This apparition you saw. It was in the open doorway—not outside in the hall?'

'It—he—was there in the doorway, Alex. I froze in horror, and for an instant I couldn't tear my eyes away. Then I screamed my head off and jumped out of bed in such a panic I actually passed out. A first for me, by the way,' she informed him, and shivered. 'I need a shower.' She licked her dry lips, eyeing him in appeal. 'Would you stay here while I'm in the bathroom?'

'Of course.' He frowned. 'But be quick, because I must search the *Kastro*. If what, or who, you saw here was real and not a dream, he must be found. I'll ring Theo.'

'*No!* Please don't,' she said, appalled. 'It was

just a dream.' Vivid and horrible, but what else could it have been?

Alex nodded reluctantly. 'As you wish.'

'Thank you, Alex.' She smiled brightly. 'Sorry for the fuss. One way or another, you'll be glad to see the back of me.'

He shook his head. 'On the contrary. My mother—as always—is right. The company of an intelligent woman is a very desirable thing.'

Her smile was ironic. 'But you must know lots of women. With your reputation and wealth and—and the rest of it—you must be beating them off with a stick!'

Alex threw back his head and laughed. 'What a picture you paint of me.' He raised an eyebrow. 'What do you mean by "the rest of it"?'

'You know very well.'

'Tell me.'

'The physique and the looks, of course,' she said irritably.

'You find me good to look at?'

She rolled her eyes. 'You know perfectly well I do.'

'You are good to look at too, Eleanor,' he said, in a tone which made her quiver. 'I stood looking at you in the sun this afternoon before you knew I was there.'

He was wrong about that. She'd known the moment he stepped onto the roof, and not just because her hearing was acute. Alexei Drakos had a way of making his presence felt.

'You made a very charming picture lying there.' His eyes lit with sudden fury. 'Then I saw the bruise at your waist and I could have strangled Spiro with my bare hands.'

Eleanor smiled shakily. 'Thank you. I think. I'll have that shower now.'

Alex got up and stood over her. 'Can you stand?'

'Yes,' she said firmly, embarrassed to find her camisole and shorts soaked with sweat. 'I'm fine now,' she said, face hot, and made for the bathroom as fast as her shaky knees would allow.

'Be quick, in case you feel faint again,' Alex ordered.

Eleanor groaned in despair at her reflection. She would have to wash her hair. She got on with it as fast as she could but, with shaking hands and legs threatening to fold under her, it took time before she was dry and wrapped in Talia's robe. She combed her hair through and swathed it in a towel then slapped moisturiser into her cheeks to bring some colour back to them. When she opened the door, Alex was eyeing the stripped bed, perplexed.

'The sheets were so damp I took them off, but where does Sofia keep the replacements?'

Eleanor crossed to the dresser and began opening drawers until she found a stack of perfectly laundered bed linen. *'Voila!'*

'Excellent! But there is still a problem. The mattress is also damp. You can't sleep here tonight.'

She cringed at the thought of drenching his mother's bed with sweat. How gross was that? 'Of course I can. Those chairs are really comfortable.'

'For sitting only. You shall sleep in my bed again.' His lips twitched at the look on her face. 'I'll take the couch in my office.'

Eleanor shook her head vehemently. 'Thank you, but that's unnecessary. I can sleep on the settee in the tower room.' Even though she quailed at the prospect. The thought of spending the night alone in any room in the apartment scared the living daylights out of her.

'No, Eleanor. You take my bed; I'll take the office couch.' He raised an eyebrow as she chuckled. 'It's good to hear you laugh, but what is funny?'

'I once worked on a paper where the boss's office couch was a way of getting a promotion for some women on the staff,' she told him.

He grinned. 'Not for you, of course.'

Eleanor batted her eyelashes. 'When it was suggested to me, I cried prettily, insisting it was against my religion to have sex before marriage. The M word frightened him so much he avoided me like the plague after that—though he gave me a glowing reference when I left. Another man glad to see the back of me!' She removed the towel and ran her fingers through her hair. 'I'll just get something else to wear.'

'Be quick, then,' he ordered. 'You need sleep. Bring your phone.'

In the bathroom Eleanor pulled on her one and only nightgown, replaced the robe and slipped the phone into her pocket. Alex held out his hand as she emerged, and she clung to it as they went along the hall, half-expecting the apparition to leap out at them until Alex closed his bedroom door behind them.

Eleanor eyed his bed with respect. 'You must be a very tidy sleeper.'

He shook his head. 'I was not in bed. I did some work in the office after you left me. I was un-dressing when I heard you scream.' He turned the covers back on one side of the bed. 'No more nightmares tonight, *parakolo,*' he commanded.

She hugged her arms across her chest. 'If it was a nightmare. He looked very real to me.'

'In which case, I should have searched for him.' Alex smiled at the look of dismay on her face. 'But I will leave it until the morning. Now get into bed.' He frowned as Eleanor hesitated. 'You're still not happy?'

'Not really, no.' She braced herself. 'Could you possibly sleep in here tonight, Alex? Please?'

His dark eyes flared for an instant before nar-rowing to the familiar, assessing look. 'Your dream frightened you that much?'

Oh yes. It had felt too real for a dream. The more she thought about it now she was calmer, the more she was convinced that the apparition had been a flesh-and-blood man—from the neck down, at least. In that second of sheer, blazing terror his image had imprinted itself on her mind so indelibly she had only to shut her eyes to see him again in every detail. Every detail… Her eyes flew open again as she turned to Alex in sudden dread. 'He had a tattoo on his arm.'

He frowned as he sat on the edge of the bed. 'Are you sure you're not remembering the dancer who played the Minotaur at the festival?'

'Absolutely sure. In my photographs he definitely has no tattoo.'

'Can you describe this?'

'No. I stared for only an instant before I screamed and passed out,' Eleanor said bitterly.

'If he's that real to you, I have no choice. I must search the *Kastro* immediately.' Alex looked suddenly older, his mouth and eyes grim as he pulled on his clothes.

She cursed herself for convincing Alex that her intruder wasn't a figment of her imagination. 'If you must, please take someone with you!'

'I am more concerned with your safety than mine, Eleanor.' His eyes softened as he sat down beside her. 'Now listen to me, *agape mou*. When I leave, lock the door and do not open it until I get back. I shall turn every light on up here on this floor. You are completely safe locked here in my room, but ring me if you need me.'

She nodded forlornly, filled with a sudden over-powering desire to go home, back where she belonged.

Alex looked down at her for a moment, then pulled her up into his arms and kissed her very thoroughly. 'Get into bed and try to sleep,' he said huskily and strode to the door with her. 'Lock the door,' he repeated his order, and closed it behind him.

Alex flicked on lights as he went along and rang Theo as he went up the stairs to the roof door to confirm it was locked. When he took the lift down to the ground floor he opened the outer door a crack at the back entrance to the *Kastro* and Theo Lazarides left his house and hurried to meet him. Alex spoke in a rapid undertone as he described his guest's nightmare and stated his intention to search the warren of ancient rooms in the Kastro basement. Theo promptly offered to accompany him, but Alex shook his head. 'Just get ready to catch him when I flush him out.'

'You think the lady really saw someone then, *kyrie*?'

'At first I was sure it was just a bad dream, but later she remembered a tattoo, so it might be possible it was not. Sorry to involve you, Theo. You must be tired.'

'Not so tired I could sleep, knowing you were searching down there alone with no one to watch your back. You think someone is lying low somewhere in the old part?'

'No, I do not. But I'm going to make sure.' Alex smiled grimly. 'I was lucky enough to achieve a meteoric success rate early on in life to get where I am now, but I'm not fool enough to believe I did it without making enemies. Someone's out to cause me pain of some kind, financial or personal, but the fool made the biggest mistake of his life when he paid someone to kidnap my mother. I'm indebted to Ms Markham for her share in preventing that, so the least I can do is make the search to ease her mind. And mine.'

Theo looked worried. 'You think this is all connected to *kyria* Talia?'

'Because it would hurt me most, yes.' Alex tested a couple of torches. 'My method of dealing with opponents has been pre-emptive all my life—to get in with my strike before they get in with theirs. I learned that very early on with all the opponents lurking along my road to success. So now I'm going to flush out this man and get rid of him before he does any more harm.'

'You think he is real, then.'

'In my head, no, but I can't take any chances, Theo.' His eyes glittered coldly. 'If he is real, I could kill the swine just for frightening my guest. And I've left Ms Markham alone up there, so I'd better get on with it.'

Theo caught his arm. 'Let me go in there with you, *kyrie*!'

'No. I appreciate the offer, but I've got more chance of catching him unawares if I go in alone.'

In time, when the reconstruction was completed, Alexei intended this oldest part of the *Kastro* to function as more storerooms for the island's produce, but in the beginning his priority had merely been making the basement structure of the place sound. Once that was done, he organised transformation of the ground floor into kitchen and living quarters, plus a personal exercise room, and went on to convert the top floor into his private apartment with offices on the floor immediately below it. Come the autumn, the majority of the male population would get to work on the network of rooms and passages in the cellars and basement.

Armed with a torch, Alex left Theo standing guard by the door which opened from the hall on to the ancient steps and descended cautiously, his deck shoes noiseless on the ancient stones picked out by the solitary beam of light.

It was eerie work, hunting a phantom quarry. But Eleanor's terror had been so genuine her scream had given him the same dread he'd felt when his mother shrieked his name as Spiro snatched her at the festival. His eyes glittered coldly. If whoever was lurking in his *Kastro* was involved in either incident, he would pay for it, and pay dearly. Alex moved silently through the familiar stone maze, feeling his way along walls which gave way to doorways and narrow passageways, until he was satisfied that even the last possible hiding place was empty. It was slow, nerve-straining work, his entire system on full alert, prepared for attack which never happened. No one was there. Cursing silently, he mounted the ancient steps, shaking his head in response to Theo's raised eyebrows as he emerged.

'It must have been a dream after all.' He shrugged. 'Ms Markham was fascinated by the bull dance, and took some extraordinary photographs. The dancer who played the Minotaur made such an impression he surfaced in her dreams.'

Theo nodded gravely. 'But you had to make sure.'

'No choice, really,' said Alex grimly. 'I object to intruders on our island.'

'Your island now, *kyrie.*'

Alex shook his head. 'Ours, Theo.'

The man smiled. '*Efcharisto*! If I can be of no more help I will go home.'

'Right.' Alex looked down at his clothes in distaste. 'I must clean up. I'll be glad when we've got the place in shape down there; it's a damned difficult job looking for someone the way it is.'

'But you came out unharmed, thank God.' Theo touched his shoulder and said goodnight.

Alex went silently to the kitchen, taking care not to disturb Sofia and the boys as he collected fruit juice and mineral water for Eleanor. Who would probably take him up on his offer to sleep in his office, now there was no danger lurking down below, or none that he'd found. Nevertheless he couldn't rid himself of the feeling of unease as he left the lift to make for his bedroom. Even though there'd been no trace of anyone lurking down below, Eleanor's account of her nightmare had been so detailed it was hard to dismiss it as nonsense. He shrugged. She'd probably seen a photograph or a painting somewhere on the Internet during her research. There'd been enough representations of the Minotaur by artists down the ages.

He knocked softly on his bedroom door. 'Alex, Eleanor.'

She flung it open, her eyes luminous with relief. 'Are you all right?'

'Dirty and thirsty, but otherwise fine.' He locked the door behind him. 'There was no sign of anyone down there, but I'd rather you stayed here with me tonight.'

So would Eleanor. She smiled gratefully as Alex put the water and juice on his dressing chest. 'You raided the kitchen, then.'

'Very stealthily, to avoid waking Sofia and the boys. Now I need a shower. I will be quick.'

Alone in the bedroom, reaction suddenly hit Eleanor in a rush of tears and chattering teeth. The strain of worrying about Alex getting injured—or worse—by the monster suddenly caught up with her. She heaved in a few deep, calming breaths as she mopped her eyes, then drank some water and curled up in the leather chair beside the bed. She smiled brightly as Alex came out of the bathroom.

'You've been crying,' he accused.

'Just a reaction. I was worried.'

He smoothed a hand over her hair. 'You are exhausted. Come to bed.'

'No thank you.' Eleanor smiled politely. 'I'll sleep here in this comfortable chair.'

His lips curved. 'I'm no threat to you tonight, *agape mou*. You've had an exhausting day and need sleep. So do I. You may sleep undisturbed. Humour me, Eleanor.' He yawned, shrugged out of his dressing gown and slid into bed. 'I can't rest with you sitting there.'

She turned out the lamp, then took off Talia's robe and got into the near side of the bed, keeping to the edge to leave as much space as possible between them.

'You'll fall on the floor in the night if you try to sleep like that,' he commented.

'I'll take the risk.'

There was silence for a while.

'Eleanor.'

'Yes?'

'I found nothing down there, so it must have been a dream. Relax. You can sleep undisturbed by monsters or anything else—including me.'

'Thank you. Goodnight, Alex.' She turned away from him and burrowed her head in the pillows, suddenly so tired she wouldn't have stirred if the creature in the bull mask had come to tuck her in.

At some point during the night Eleanor woke to find she was alone in the bed and light coming from the bathroom. Alex opened the door and stood looking at her.

'I disturbed you.' He switched off the bathroom light and got back into bed.

Eleanor flushed in the darkness. This enforced intimacy was hard to take. Tomorrow night she would sleep in Talia's bed and sleep well with no danger of a monster lurking in her doorway. As there never had been. She felt hideously embarrassed about getting in such a state over a nightmare. Screaming her head off, sweating with fear and, top of the bill, fainting like a maiden in a Victorian novel.

'You cannot sleep?' said a drowsy voice.

'Sorry to keep you awake.' She gasped as a hard arm snaked round her waist and pulled her across the bed.

'Lie still,' Alex muttered, and settled her comfortably against him.

She obeyed, waiting motionless until he relaxed his grasp so she could escape. But Alex's arm stayed firmly in place, holding her fast as he slept. Eleanor yawned, blinking hard. Heavens she was tired...

When she woke again, heart pounding, she was held close to Alex's chest.

'You were making little cries in your sleep,' Alex told her in a tone that set all her alarm bells ringing. 'Were you dreaming?'

'Probably, but nothing scary this time. At least, not that I can remember.' She stirred restlessly, but his hold tightened. He smoothed his cheek against hers, turning her face until their lips met in a kiss so gentle it disarmed her. As it was meant to, the still-functioning part of her brain warned her. His mouth caressed hers until her lips parted to his insistent tongue as he held her so tightly she could feel him hardening against her. She stifled a moan at the touch of seducing hands which ignited her into arousal, heightened by the emotions of the night. He smothered her half-hearted protest with kisses as he dispensed with her nightgown, and sent his mouth roving lower. She choked back a groan as his mouth closed over a hard, sensitive nipple while his fingers caressed its twin and sent fire streaking through her body right down to her toes, disposing of her resistance as his free hand slid between her thighs.

When his seeking fingers found the evidence of her response, she was suddenly a wild thing in his arms. He crushed his lips to hers as he moved over her and into her, then held her tight in pulsing possession for several glorious seconds before his body urged hers into a rhythm which rapidly accelerated into a wild, gasping ascent towards a peak of pleasure he reached alone. He stiffened in the throes of his release as he left her stranded and breathless, the magnificent body heavy as lead on her bruised ribs when it collapsed on hers.

Eleanor pushed at his shoulders. 'You're squashing me,' she hissed, and with a groan he heaved himself away to look down into her flushed, none-too-happy face.

'Forgive me,' he said, surprising her.

Her eyes glittered coldly. 'If a man wakes up in the night with a woman in his arms—any woman—the result is inevitable. I should have gone back to the other room, but I was too scared.'

'The apology,' he informed her formally, 'Was for my haste.'

'Don't worry about it,' she said airily. 'The hassle of searching for the intruder obviously affected your performance.' She searched for her nightgown, her face hot as she came in contact with a bare, muscular leg. 'May I use your shower now, please?'

'You need to ask?'

'Yes!'

'You're angry.'

'Yes to that, too.'

'Because I was too rushed?'

'No!'

'Then because you feel I forced you, Eleanor?'

Eleanor shook her head. 'You know perfectly well that you didn't force me. You're so skilled at the foreplay stuff I had no chance from the start.

I'm angry with myself for giving in so easily.' She pulled on the dressing gown and switched on the lamp to find Alex surveying her with narrowed, brooding eyes.

'You need have no worries, Eleanor,' he informed her.

'Splendid. None for you, either. I use birth control, so there won't be any embarrassing little outcome.'

'It would not be embarrassing for me! If there was a child, I would care for it. I was reassuring you about my sexual health.' He chuckled as she flushed. 'You are a surprising lady, Eleanor. You discuss the possibility of an illegitimate child so calmly, yet on the subject of health pitfalls you blush.'

She pushed a strand of hair behind her ear. 'I wasn't blushing. I went hot because that was a risk I hadn't thought of!'

'You need think of it no longer.'

'Splendid.' She caught her breath as Alex leaned to seize her hand, and kissed each finger very deliberately.

'Why so hostile?'

'Stop trying to distract me,' she snapped, eyes flashing like danger signals as he laughed.

'So tell me, Eleanor Markham, if the man you lusted after had returned your feelings, would you have married him?'

'Oh yes, like a shot—at the time. But that was years ago.' She smiled brightly. 'I was soon deeply grateful to him for marrying someone else. And now I'm going to shower, and then I'll spend the rest of the night in that chair.'

Alex took over the bathroom after Eleanor emerged, and frowned when he came out at the sight of her curled up in the chair with a pillow.

'Come back to bed, Eleanor. You need sleep, and so do I. And neither of us will achieve that if you sit up all night.' He smiled persuasively. 'I promise to let you sleep in peace.'

She shook her head. 'I'll keep to the chair. Pretend I'm not here.'

'As if I could possibly do that!' His eyes were sombre as he got into bed. 'You will be leaving soon, but I think you are unlikely to forget your stay on Kyrkiros, Eleanor.'

'You're absolutely right. I actually achieved an interview with Alexei Drakos.'

He scowled. 'Is that all you will remember?'

'Of course not. I also had the great good fortune to meet your mother.'

'And had so bad a nightmare you fainted,' he reminded her, eyes darkening. 'When I found you unconscious on the floor, my heart stopped.'

She shivered a little. 'Then it's high time you got some sleep to recover.'

'In the morning I shall take you to see a little of my island,' he said, and smiled. 'I feel confident it's no longer necessary to hide you away.'

'I'll enjoy that very much. Will you let me take photographs? Not for my column. I just want souvenirs of my time here, Alex.'

'To remind you of me?'

She smiled sadly. 'I doubt I'll need reminders, Alexei.' She closed her eyes very deliberately and turned her head into the pillow.

'You can't sleep like that and neither can I.' He slid out of bed to sink to his knees in front of her. 'Come back to bed. I shall stay here like this until you do.'

Eleanor stared into the glittering dark eyes locked on hers. 'That's blackmail.'

'I know!'

'Oh—very well.' He was right, not that she was going to admit it. The chair was less comfortable than it looked.

Alex got up, holding out his hand, but Eleanor shook her head, picked up her pillow and resumed her former place on the edge. Without a word he turned out the light and got into bed on the far side, and then leaned back against his pillows, so utterly still it was impossible for her to relax because she kept expecting that arm to reach out and draw her close again. She wanted it to, she realised, heart sinking. What a fool! In a couple of days she would be home again, back in the real world, in her humdrum life. And, back in his anything but humdrum life, Alexei Drakos would forget about her the moment her plane took off.

'I shall miss you,' he said as though he'd read her mind.

She blinked. 'You haven't known me long enough to miss me.'

'Our acquaintance has not been long,' he agreed and laughed softly. 'But it has been so memorable I will never forget you, Eleanor.'

'Good to know I made such an impression.'

'While I have made a very bad impression on you.'

'Only in the beginning. You made up for that with the interview.'

'Could you forget the damned interview? I meant my love-making.'

Heat rushed, unseen, to Eleanor's face. 'Don't talk about it any more. You should sleep.'

'Hold my hand and I will.'

With a sigh Eleanor turned onto her back and stretched out her hand. He grasped it in his, then very slowly he drew her across the space between them and into his arms, holding her against his chest with her head on his shoulder.

'This is good, *ne*?'

'Yes.'

'Can you sleep like this?'

'No.'

'You want to go back to the other side?'

'No.'

His arms tightened. 'You feel almost perfect in my arms, Eleanor.'

'Almost?'

'If I tell you how to make it perfect you will go back to that chair,' he whispered into her hair.

'No I won't. You were right. I couldn't have slept there.'

'Why not?'

Oh, to hell with it, she thought, suddenly reckless. 'Because I want to be here with you.'

Alex tipped her face up to his and kissed her fiercely, and with a purring sound she kissed him back, running a caressing hand down his bare chest.

'You have changed your mind?' he said unevenly.

'Yes.'

'Why?'

'Because life is short and this will never happen again.' She smiled up into his taut face, glorying in the fact that his chest was rising and falling rapidly as she caressed it. 'Now tell me how to make it perfect. Or perhaps I can guess.' She sat up and took the nightgown over her head. 'Is that what you had in mind?'

'Exactly,' he agreed, the look in his eyes as tactile as a caress.

'Now you!'

He promptly threw his only garment away with such drama, Eleanor laughed.

'You laugh at me?' he demanded, crushing her to him.

'Not at you—with you. I do so admire a grand gesture!'

He grinned, and then sobered, looking down at her in wonder.

'What's wrong?'

'Nothing, *glykia mou*. Everything is suddenly, wonderfully right.' He kissed her, taking his time over it, nibbling at the bottom lip then licking around the edge of her lips before kissing them with a sigh which melted her completely. He raised his head to smile at her. 'I have made love to women before.'

'Really bad time to mention it,' she warned, eyes flashing.

He laughed, rubbing his cheek against hers, and then nipped at her lips with fierce, plucking kisses. 'I mention it because with you it is different.'

'I bet you say that to all the girls!'

'*Ochi*! I do not. You are different because I can

laugh with you—even though I want you so much it is hard to breathe.'

Eleanor buried her face against him and held him close, glorying in the drumbeat of his heart against her as she pressed hot, open-mouthed kisses over his chest, licking at him with the tip of her tongue until he turned her face up to his and took her open mouth in a kiss of rough possession which thrilled her down to her toes.

He tore his mouth away and buried his face in her hair. 'This time,' he said huskily, 'I will not give way to greed and rush. I want—I *need*—you to share the glory I found with you earlier.'

'Is it a matter of pride to bring a woman to orgasm every time?' she asked, and he shook with laughter.

'Since you ask, clinical one, yes it is. But it is more a desire to share my pleasure than pride.' He tipped her face up to his. 'Do your lovers leave you wanting sometimes?'

She bit her lip, eyeing him under her lashes. 'I don't think of them as lovers.'

'It does not surprise me if they leave you unsatisfied!'

'None of the men in my past fitted the description, exactly.'

Alex held her closer. 'How many?'

'Hundreds!' Eleanor laughed at the look on his face. 'Only teasing, more like one or two. Since I started in my present job, relationships are hard work because I travel so much. I met my first boyfriend in school, but we were too young for the sex thing, I suppose.'

His arms tightened around her. 'Teenage boys are walking hormones, Eleanor. I speak from experience. He would have wanted sex!'

She shook her head. 'He was too wrapped up in his work. He was totally focused on doing well in exams. He never wanted sex with me.'

'I don't want sex, either,' Alex said, startling her. The evidence that he did was hard to miss.

'Let's go to sleep then.'

'Not yet. First, *glykia mou,* we make love.'

'You said you didn't want that.'

He tipped her face up to his and kissed her. 'I said I didn't want sex. That is just a mindless, mechanical meeting of bodies, *ne*? To achieve true rapture, the mind and spirit must be involved.'

But not the heart. Eleanor and ran a questing finger down his chest. 'Show me, then.'

This time Alex lingered so long over making love to every part of her Eleanor was trembling and impatient and almost reduced to tears before his body joined with hers. The blissful sensation of union was so intense they achieved instant perfect rhythm, which threatened to hurtle them towards climax far too soon. But this time Alex took her to the brink and held her there several tantalising times before she came apart in his arms at last, and with a visceral groan he surrendered to his own release, his face buried in her hair.

Eleanor was happy to have Alex stay where he was. By some strange alchemy his weight was easy to bear this time. She revelled in the feeling of the graceful, muscular body still joined with hers in the ultimate intimacy, his arms still holding her close. One of them ought to move, but since it obviously wasn't going to be her she was content to stay where she was and enjoy the experience to the full. As Alex had promised, it had been no mere mechanical process. Making love with him had transcended anything she'd experienced before. Alex raised his head and smiled down into eyes which widened in surprise as she felt him harden inside her.

'I want you again, *kardia mou*,' he said huskily in a tone which caused such a melting sensation inside her he thrust deeper to take advantage of it. 'You want me too, *ne*?'

When he kissed her she responded wildly, her body saying yes without words as he began to make love to her all over again, but this time faster and wilder, as she met him thrust for thrust until they gasped together in the throes of culmination so overwhelming it left them speechless in each other's arms. It was a long time before Alex reluctantly separated from her. He slid from the bed, holding out his hand and, feeling irrationally shy, Eleanor took it and let him draw her to her feet.

'We shall shower together and then sleep together, *ne*?'

She nodded silently, thrilled to her toes when Alex picked her up and carried her into the bathroom. He set her down very gently in the shower stall and turned on the water, waited until it warmed and drew her into his arms to stand under the spray.

'We must not stay here like this together very long or I will want you again!'

Eleanor stared at him, astonished. 'Really?'

'Really!' He soaped her with caresses which proved it was no idle threat, and she laughed and pushed him away while she rinsed.

'I would like a towel please,' she said primly.

'You Brits are so cold-blooded,' he mocked, and then leapt away, laughing as her eyes flashed. 'Shall I help you get dry, *agapi mou*?'

She shook her head, stifling a yawn as she swathed herself in the towel. 'I'll do it so we get back to bed faster. I'm tired, *kyrie* Drakos.'

'Which is no surprise,' he said, drying off quickly. 'After enduring storms and nightmares and my love-making, it is only natural you are tired.' He took her hand and led her back into the bedroom. He tidied the bed a little then got into it and held out his arms. Eleanor gave her hair one last rub, turned out the light, slid into Alex's embrace and with a murmur of pleasure he pulled her close and drew up the covers.

'I didn't *endure* your love-making,' she said sleepily.

He rubbed his cheek against hers. 'You liked it?'

Eleanor raised her head to smile at him. 'I loved it.'

He kissed her gently and smoothed her head back down against his shoulder. 'In the morning we shall swim together, Eleanor.'

She sighed happily. 'Yes, Alex.'

'Now sleep.'

'Yes, Alex.'

He chuckled and held her close as he gazed into the darkness. Just one more day and Miss Eleanor Markham would be gone. And so would he. His stay on Kyrkiros had been longer than intended and now it was time to stop lotus-eating and get back to the real world which provided the means to go on with the work planned on the island. But, before spending time on the beach with Eleanor, he would take another look in the Kastro basement. Then after their swim he would take her on a short tour of the island and touch base with as many inhabitants as possible.

CHAPTER EIGHT

ELEANOR'S interior alarm woke her early enough to let her pull on the bathrobe and unlock the door before Alex caught her in his arms.

'Where are you going?'

'Back to my room before Sofia finds I'm missing.'

He pushed the tousled curls back from his face and kissed her at such length they were both breathless when he let her go. 'Come back to bed,' he whispered, but Eleanor found the strength from somewhere to shake her head.

'The bed will be dry by now in my room.' She smiled ruefully. 'Humour me. I want to make it up with fresh linen before Sofia arrives.'

Alex laughed indulgently. 'If you must, you must, Eleanor Markham.' He glanced at his watch. 'But Sofia will not be here for half an hour yet.'

'In that case, we can sort your bed out before I go.'

And, no matter how much he laughed, Eleanor insisted on restoring Alex's bed to some semblance of order, demanding his help to plump up pillows and turn down the covers.

'Good,' she said with satisfaction afterwards and made for the door. 'Now I can do mine.'

'Shall I come and help?'

She shook her head, smiling. 'Think how shocked Sofia would be.'

Alex ruffled her hair. 'Be quick, then. I shall come for you when breakfast is ready.'

In the bright light of day Eleanor's fears seemed so silly as she hurried to her room, she bitterly regretted sending Alex off on a wild-goose chase. To her relief the mattress had dried overnight, but to be on the safe side she did some hauling and pushing and turned it over before putting the clean linen on it. When she was satisfied it looked pristine and perfect in its white covers, she got into a black one-piece swimsuit, added shorts and T-shirt and did some work on her hair and face, faintly surprised to find she looked much the same as usual. Eleanor laughed at herself in the mirror. Had she really expected a night of love to show on her face? There were one or two suspicious marks on her skin, but a touch of concealer soon remedied that. If she'd been alone she'd have left them as evidence that, although she'd dreamed about a monster, Alex's love-making had been hot, sweet reality.

When the expected knock came on her door Eleanor threw it open to find Sofia smiling at her.

'*Kalimera, kyria.*'

'*Kalimera,* Sofia, how is Yannis?'

Yannis, she was informed, was much better this morning, due to the *kyria's* medicine, and now he was eating a big breakfast. The woman patted Eleanor's hand gratefully. 'You are a very kind lady. *Kyrie* Alexei is waiting for you.'

Eleanor thanked her and walked with her to the lift, then ran to the tower room when she saw Alex in the doorway. He kissed her hand and held out a chair for her at the table.

'I'm hungry,' he informed her.

'So am I!' Eleanor surveyed the array of fruit and freshly baked rolls with anticipation.

'Love has given you an appetite?'

Love? She was proud of her steady hand as she poured coffee into his cup. 'Yes. Though it can sometimes do the reverse.'

'When this idiot friend of your rejected you as a lover?' he said instantly and took her hand. 'He was a fool to miss the glory of making love with you.'

'Thank you.' She buttered a roll and ate half of it as she tried, and failed, to picture Dominic Hall making love to her with even a fraction of Alex's skill.

Alex eyed her accusingly. 'You are thinking of him?'

'Yes. I realised an experience like last night would never have been possible with him,' she said candidly.

'It would not have been as good as with me?' he said, reaching out a hand to touch hers.

Eleanor curled her fingers round his. 'No.'

Alex gave her the smile that made her heart turn cartwheels. 'Good. Now, eat. And then we swim.' He passed his cup over. 'More coffee, *parakolo*.'

Eleanor's eyes lingered on his sun-burnished hair, and strong, sculpted features. *You can have anything in the world you want,* she thought as she refilled his cup. Yet in two days she would be back in the UK and would never see him again. She blinked the thought away. Until she left to catch her plane, she must make the most of every moment left of this unique, never-to-be-repeated experience. Alexei Drakos, philanthropist and entrepreneur, was so far out of her league it would have been better in some ways if last night had never happened. Making love with him had been as life-altering as expected—and feared. No other man would ever compare.

'You are day-dreaming,' Alex stated, his eyes kindling. 'What were you thinking about?'

'You.'

'So honest.' He got to his feet and pulled her out of her chair and into his arms to kiss her. 'You are a new experience in my life, Eleanor Markham.'

'Ditto, Alexei Drakos!'

He held her closer. 'Stay longer.'

She shook her head regretfully. 'I need to get back to reality. And you're overdue at whatever destination you were making for after the festival.'

'They can wait for me,' he said with careless arrogance.

'But my job won't wait for me. As Ross McLean constantly informs me, there are dozens of others eager to step into my shoes.'

Alex made a chopping motion with his hand. 'If he gives you trouble, I will take care of him.'

Eleanor found Alex in this mood a big surprise. The love-making in the night might have been the most thrilling experience of *her* life but, sure it was the norm for him, she had expected him to revert to his former persona this morning. To find him behaving like a lover was delightful but unnerving.

'Thank you for the thought, but I can deal with Ross. I thought we were going for a swim,' she added.

He frowned. 'I should search the *Kastro* basement again first.'

'Surely that's unnecessary? You found nothing last night.' She looked him in the eye. 'It will take you too long. I'll be gone tomorrow, remember.'

'You think I have forgotten that?' He took her hand. 'As you wish. I will ask Theo to keep everyone away from my beach, so that I can have you all to myself. How long will you be?'

'Ten minutes.'

He laughed. 'Which means half an hour, *ne*?'

'No, it means ten minutes!'

'Let's make a wager. What will you give me if—when—you lose?'

'My apologies,' she said, laughing, and took off down the hall to her room.

After her period of virtual captivity Eleanor found it so good to be out in the sun with Alex, she felt like singing as he helped her down a steep path to a triangle of sand enclosed in complete privacy by sheltering rocks, softened by shrubs and greenery.

'You keep this entirely to yourself, Alex?'

He shook a towel out for her to sit on. 'Only when I'm here. Otherwise all are welcome to use it.'

'Ah, but do they?' Eleanor leaned back against her tote bag.

'I've never asked.' He took off his shirt and let himself down beside her with a sigh of pleasure. 'I'm happy to help you with your sun lotion.' He stroked a hand along her thigh.

'I put it on before we came out.'

'A pity. I would have enjoyed smoothing it over your skin.'

Eleanor quivered inside and cast a look at the

graceful, muscular body stretched out beside her. 'I could put some on you, if you like.'

Alex laughed. 'I would like it far too much! Perhaps you could do that later when we are alone in my room.'

So he expected her to sleep with him again tonight. 'No need for sun block at night!'

'True. But I would delight in the touch of your hands on me, *glykia mou.*'

Eleanor frowned at him. 'Time to swim,' she said gruffly and got up to remove her jeans and shirt. 'Come on.'

When she took off at a run he laughed and chased after her. She waded into the waves until she was deep enough to dive under them and he dove in after her, swimming stroke for stroke with her, then disappearing to come up alongside her to splash her. She laughed in delight and retaliated, enjoying this new playful Alex so much she was sorry when he said it was time to return to the beach.

'Otherwise you will get tired,' he said as they swam back at a leisurely rate. 'And I must take a walk. Will you come with me?'

Eleanor stood up when her feet touched bottom,

and pushed her wet hair back from her face. 'I'd like that very much.' She took the hand he held out. 'It's so lovely here, Alex. How old would you say the island is?'

'It was first inhabited about 3500 BC,' he informed her and laughed at her look of awe. 'Come, water nymph, we must get back to the Kastro to dress and then take our walk before it gets too hot.'

Later, in a raspberry-pink sun dress she'd packed as the only alternative to the ill-fated Breton number, Eleanor went along to knock on the office door to tell Alex she was ready.

'Will I do?' she asked.

'Oh yes,' he said, giving her a leisurely top-to-toe scrutiny. 'You will do perfectly. We will walk just up to the church and back, so that you can get an idea of how people live here.'

Eleanor decided against carrying her tote bag, which looked battered after its adventure as an assault weapon. She slung her camera over her shoulder instead, put on her sunglasses and white cotton hat and smiled up at Alex. 'I'm ready.'

They went into the kitchen on their way out and found Yannis helping his mother now his friend

Markos had gone home. The youth smiled shyly at Eleanor as he thanked her for the medicine, and assured *kyrie* Alexei that he was now much better.

His mother added her thanks and complimented Eleanor on her dress, then announced that lunch was cold today and could be served at whatever time it was required.

'*Efcharisto,* Sofia,' said Alex, and told her they would not be long in case the sun was too hot for *kyria* Eleanor.

'Isn't life strange?' Eleanor remarked as they set off up the steep, *maquis*-scented road together. 'I first arrived here just a couple of days ago, yet it feels a lot longer than that.'

'Because so much has happened since.' Alex smiled down at her with a warmth Eleanor marvelled at when she remembered his original hostility.

'Stop a moment; I want some shots of the houses climbing the hill up here.' She took out her camera and focused on the small houses, some of them white, others painted ochre or sky-blue, most of them with bougainvillaea tumbling over their porches in bright cascades. A woman came out of one to greet them, and Alex smiled at her and introduced his companion as a visitor from England.

'Would you ask her permission to take a photograph?' asked Eleanor.

Alex spoke to the woman, who nodded eagerly as Eleanor posed her against the white of the house and vibrant pink of the flowers to take her shot. From then on someone came out to greet them at every house as they made their way up to the blue-crowned dome of the white church, where Eleanor took a last photograph before putting her camera away.

'I would have liked to show you the vineyards, but it would take too long,' Alex told her as they turned back. 'You must come back some day to see the rest of the island.'

Never going to happen, Eleanor thought sadly.

Alex peered under the brim of the hat as they walked down the hill. 'What are you thinking?'

'I won't be sent back to this part of the world again,' she said with regret. 'My next assignment will be in the UK, researching places for unusual weekend country-breaks.'

'Then you must come back here on vacation,

with no work involved,' he said promptly, as though it was the easiest thing in the world.

'Kyrkiros isn't a holiday destination,' she reminded him.

Alex laughed softly. 'You are always welcome to share my bed, Eleanor Markham.'

'I'll keep that in mind,' she said, her voice neutral to cover the leap in her blood at the thought. When they paused for Eleanor to record the boats drawn up on the beach, Theo Lazarides came to meet them.

'Be warned, Theo,' said Alex, grinning, 'Ms Markham probably wants your photograph to add to the hundreds she's already taken this morning.'

'May I, Mr Lazarides?' said Eleanor, and when he nodded cheerfully she took a shot quickly before he could strike a stiff pose. *'Efcharisto poli.'*

'You look warm, Eleanor,' said Alex. 'Go in and tell Sofia we're ready to lunch in fifteen minutes. I need a word with Theo.'

Eleanor went up the steps into the dark, cool interior of the *Kastro*, gave Sofia the message and then took the lift to her room. She transferred the morning's photographs to her laptop and sent an email to her parents before joining Alex in the tower room, where Sofia was setting out a traditional Greek salad to eat with bread she'd baked that morning, and fresh figs for dessert.

'Where have you been, Eleanor?' he asked.

She explained. 'My parents will meet me at the airport.'

'*Kyria* Eleanor will be leaving us tomorrow, Sofia.' Alex told the woman.

'Then I will make a special dinner tonight,' she promised and smiled sadly at Eleanor. 'It is a pity you must leave, *kyria*. You must come back soon.'

Eleanor smiled brightly. 'Perhaps for next year's festival.'

'You didn't mean that,' said Alex when they were alone.

'No. Ross was too grudging about the expenses for this trip to want something similar any time soon. Besides...' She paused and helped herself to salad.

'Besides?' he prompted.

Eleanor looked at him steadily. 'This has been the kind of unique experience that never happens twice.'

'Never is a long time,' he said, returning the look. 'Who knows what fate has in store for us?'

She smiled and went on eating, but abandoned the meal after only a few mouthfuls and drank some water.

'You are not hungry?' Alex asked.

'Not very.'

'I took you too far in the heat.' He helped her to some figs. 'Eat some of these to give you energy, then rest on your bed—alone,' he added and touched a fingertip to her bottom lip. 'This afternoon I must go out for a while to the vineyards.'

'I'd rather go up to the roof and make the most of this sunshine before I go.'

Alex patted her hand. 'You may do whatever you wish, *glykia mou*. But don't stay up there too long. If you are not back in your room when I return, I will come and fetch you.'

Eleanor's eyes sparkled. 'Is that a promise?'

For answer he stood up and snatched her out of her chair to kiss her. 'Or I could stay and not go at all,' he whispered, his breath hot against her neck.

'Never let it be said I took you away from your responsibilities,' she said primly and with effort moved out of his arms. 'You go and do your thing. I shall have my final sunbathe, and then this evening—'

'We shall go to bed after dinner to enjoy every minute of our last night together,' he said emphatically, and smiled into her eyes. 'You agree with me?'

Eleanor flushed. 'You know I do.' She began putting the remains of their meal in the trolley and smiled in approval as Alex helped. 'Well done. I'm having such a good influence on you.'

'Very true.' The dark eyes met hers with intensity that quickened her pulse. 'It was my great good fortune that your Ross McLean sent you to interview me.'

'Not *quite* your original reaction,' she retorted, her tone tart to hide her delight.

'No, *kyria* journalist, it was not! But now it is hard for me to part with you for just an hour.'

This statement pleased her so much, she reached up to kiss him.

He looked down at her in surprise. 'You kissed me.'

'You didn't like it?'

He seized her in his arms. 'Of course I liked it, but until now I have done the kissing.'

'I always kiss you back,' she said breathlessly and gave him a wry little smile. 'I can't help it.

You kiss me and I'm lost—which,' she added, pulling away from him, 'Is not the cleverest thing to admit.'

'I disagree. It is exactly what a lover wants to hear,' he assured her as they went along the hall and smiled as her eyes opened wide. 'I will prove it to you later,' he assured her, then kissed her and opened the door to her room. 'I must go. Do not stay up on the roof too long.'

'Are you getting to your vineyards by boat?'

Alex shook his head. 'I keep an off-road vehicle here on the island.' He strode off to the lift and waved a hand to her as the doors opened. '*Antia, glykia mou.*'

CHAPTER NINE

ELEANOR soon settled under a parasol in the roof garden, but found it so hard to concentrate on the not very thrilling plot she put her book down, feeling tired. The last couple of days had made such demands on her stamina, a short nap was necessary since she was unlikely to get much sleep tonight. Stretching like a cat in the sun at the thought, she woke later, yawning, to find she'd been asleep for more than an hour. She put her belongings in her bag and crossed over to the balustrade to gaze at the sun glittering on the sea, turned away to take a last look at the roof garden and with a sigh went down the stairs into the relative dimness of the hall. A hard arm closed round her, and she smiled in the split second before a gag was thrust in her mouth and she found her captor wasn't Alex.

She gave smothered sounds of violent protest and fought wildly, kicking out as her hands were wrenched behind her back, but she stopped dead when a knife was brandished before her startled eyes. Afraid to move as her wrists were tied cruelly tight, she was jerked round to face a man with a pelt of close-cut black curls above a broad, low-browed face, his eyes glittering with such menace Eleanor abandoned all idea of struggling in case he set to work with his knife. He slung her bag over his shoulder, and with a torch in one hand seized her arm with the other to hurry her down the old, spiral stone stairs.

When they reached the hall level he stopped, cursing in a vicious undertone at the sound of car doors slamming and voices outside. Eleanor tried to make a break for it, but he jerked her back and hauled her down into the labyrinthine depths of the old *Kastro* at such breakneck speed she was in constant fear of spraining an ankle as she tried to undo the clasp of her bracelet without her captor noticing. Her relief was intense when the chain slipped from her wrist as her captor chivvied her on a dizzying route along passageways, down flights of steps and finally thrust her into a cave-like space with a narrow aperture which let in just enough light for her to see him heave a tall stone across the opening.

Her captor pushed her to a stone ledge, his hand heavy on her shoulder to force her to sit. Head throbbing and heart knocking against her ribs, Eleanor glared at the man furiously, hoping her eyes were giving off the sparks Alex liked so much. Alex! *Please* let him find the bracelet and come looking for her. She clenched her teeth against rising nausea, but the final bout of rough handling had been the last straw. Eleanor's stomach gave such a sickening lurch she began to heave, and in panic made smothered sounds of desperate entreaty. He scowled at her, but after a moment's indecision tore the gag from her mouth. She took in a great gulp of musty air, willing her stomach to behave as he spoke roughly to her.

'Don't understand,' she gasped, swallowing convulsively. 'I'm British.'

He gaped, thunderstruck.

She nodded feverishly. 'I'm a journalist. Here to report on the festival.'

He shook his head angrily. 'Speak slow.'

Eleanor repeated the words slowly and deliberately, but the man shook his head in sneering disbelief.

'Alexei Drakos never speak to reporters. You are lovers, *ne?*'

'No.' She tried to roll her shoulders. 'Please—could you untie my wrists? My shoulders are painful.'

He snorted derisively. 'You think me fool?'

'You can tie my hands again in front of me. *Parakolo?*'

He picked up the knife, his eyes gloating as he waved it in front of her face. 'You scream, I cut.'

Eleanor nodded mutely and sat very still as he untied the ropes, but to her shame couldn't stifle a groan as the blood rushed back into her shoulder muscles and sore wrists.

'*Entaxei*,' he grunted and yanked the wrists together in front of her to tie them again. He went to the doorway to move the stone a little then turned to her. 'Quiet, so I can surprise Alexei when he comes to rescue.' He slashed the knife in front of his throat in graphic illustration then slithered through the narrow opening.

Eleanor set to work to loosen her bonds, but after a fruitless interval with only her teeth as tools she gave up torturing her sore wrists to study the ancient stone block walling her in. There were depressions on it which provided natural hand-holds for manoeuvring, so when Alex had been searching down here in the dark it must have looked like part of a wall instead of an opening into this cave-like cell. Yet Eleanor was sure her captor was no thug. She had an idea he spoke better English than he was letting on. But he definitely wasn't the man in the bull mask. He was bigger, and there was no tattoo on his forearm. He looked—and smelt—too clean to have been hiding out in this grubby little cave; and his tension was palpable. Something had obviously gone wrong with this kidnap plan too.

Eleanor looked up at the stone ceiling and clenched her teeth against rising panic at the thought of the weight of centuries over her head. She had to calm down. A pounding headache and sore shoulders and wrists were trouble enough without claustrophobia—another fine Greek word! She tensed as the stone was pushed aside far enough to let her captor slither back into the room.

He gave her what was obviously meant to be an

intimidating glare. 'Alexei come soon. No scream before I say!'

'Oh please,' she said with disdain. 'You speak better English than that.'

He scowled, taken aback, and shook his head. 'You mistake.'

'No. The mistake is yours.' She pointed to his watch. 'If you want to keep the act, lose the Rolex and expensive clothes. So, tell me, who was the man in the bull mask?'

He thrust a hand through his dark curls, scowling. 'It was I.'

She shook her head. 'Right grammar, wrong answer. He had a tattoo.'

He leaned against the wall, looking sulky. 'He said you fainted.'

'I did. But I noted the tattoo first.' Eleanor winced as she shrugged her aching shoulders. 'I'm a journalist. It's my job to note details.'

'You have habit of annoying me, lady. Because of you, Spiro failed to kidnap *kyria* Talia.' He sneered. 'Alexei must be *so* grateful to you.'

Eleanor's eyes narrowed. 'You know him well, then.'

'Too well.' He shrugged and looked at his watch.

'I heard him talking up there. Our hero will soon rush to the rescue and I will overpower him.'

Eleanor's heart contracted. The thought of Alex off his guard and vulnerable to whatever weapons this psychopath had on hand was unbearable. 'Tell me,' she said conversationally, 'Why do you hate him so much?'

A tide of angry colour suffused his astonished face as he yanked her to her feet by her sore wrists. 'I have reasons.'

She eyed him defiantly to hide how much he'd hurt her. 'Did you actually intend to harm Alexei's mother before you exchanged her for ransom money?'

'*Ochi*, I do not hurt women of her age.' His hands tightened on her shoulders. 'Taking her was just the best way to hurt Alexei.' He took in a deep breath and then smiled with a relish that sent shivers down Eleanor's spine. 'But I will enjoy conquering *you*, *kyria*.'

She yanked herself away. 'Keep your filthy hands off me!'

He laughed reluctantly. 'You have spirit, English woman. Yet Markos said you fainted with fright when he appeared in the mask.'

Markos? Yannis' friend? Eleanor eyed the man disdainfully. 'Is he the puppet-master, giving you orders?'

Eyes blazing, he pushed her back down on the ledge. 'No man gives me orders,' he hissed in fury. 'Markos is ignorant boy, but useful because poor. I gave him money to buy costume from the dancers.'

'Why?'

'To wear it to scare you into coming down to his friend's boat to bring you to me on Karpyros. But he scared you too much. Our hero rushed to your rescue when you fainted, so Markos ran away and hid the mask.' He looked at his watch. 'Alexei knows now that you are missing. When he comes, scream for help to bring him to me. If not,' he added, fingering the knife, 'I will enjoy hurting you until you do.' His mouth twisted in a cynical sneer. 'The gods sent Talia Kazan to me on Karpyros that day. I was so kind—I brought her over here in my boat because Takis was busy.'

'Why?'

'Because when I saw her I had inspiration,' he said with satisfaction. 'I would pay someone to kidnap Alexei's beloved mother during the festival when no one would notice. Then I would hide her on my boat and demand ransom from him.' He glared at her. 'But you spoiled my plan. So now you pay. And Alexei will pay to get you back.'

'If you want money from Alexei, you won't get any by harming me,' Eleanor pointed out, her calm infuriating him. She changed tack and gave him a bright, social smile. 'My name's Eleanor Markham, by the way. What's yours?'

His thick black brows shot together in anger. 'You make fun of me?'

'Not at all. What *is* your name?'

'Marinos,' he said proudly.

Eleanor's eyebrows rose. 'Are you related to Alexei's college friend, Ari?'

His eyes narrowed. 'You know that?'

'Alexei mentioned a holiday spent on Crete with her.'

'At my family home, where everyone *love* Alexei. Christina most of all.'

Christina? Eleanor eyed him curiously. 'Who is she?'

'She was my girlfriend, but when she saw Alexei she wanted *him*.' His fists clenched. 'Christina followed him round like pet dog. She was furious when my sister would not take us with them when she went sailing with Alexei that day, but glad later when Arianna almost died because Drakos lost control of the dinghy when the weather changed. It was only by Poseidon's will that they were rescued, but then Alexei abandoned Arianna, and I swore to avenge her.'

His eyes lit with a maniacal gleam. 'When Arianna married Dion Aristides, Christina seized her chance to comfort Alexei, but when he tired of her she took revenge with the lies she told reporter about him. Now I will get mine.'

'It's taken you an amazingly long time to get round to it!' For a moment Eleanor thought she'd gone too far as he raised a hand to strike her, but his arm dropped and he cocked his head to listen to sounds she'd talked her head off to distract him from. 'I suppose Alexei is a hard man to get at with his security staff and his constant travelling—'

'Silence,' he spat at her, glaring. 'Our hero is near. So keep very quiet until I give order to scream.' He seized her wrist and brandished the knife. 'Or I cut one of your fingers off as gift for Alexei.'

Eleanor's stomach objected to the idea so much she sat motionless.

'Eleanor?' yelled Alex in the distance.

'He has a knife!' she screamed at the top of her voice and gave a choked cry as a fist back-handed her across the jaw.

'And I will use it to mark your whore,' roared Marinos in English,

'How stupid! You won't get money out of him that way,' Eleanor sneered at him in such derision, Marinos bellowed with rage and lunged at her, but she held him off with her joined hands and kneed him viciously in the place that hurt him most. She overbalanced and fell in a heap as Marinos doubled up, retching, and then the stone was wrenched aside with an axe and Alexei leapt in to pull Eleanor to her feet.

'Are you hurt?' he asked harshly.

She held up her bound hands. 'My wrists are sore— Look out!' She dodged back as Marinos staggered up, knife upraised, but Alex caught his wrist in an iron grip, twisting until the knife fell, clattering to the floor.

'Still fighting dirty, little brother?' Alex said

scornfully and threw a look at Eleanor over his shoulder. 'Go outside to Theo.'

'So the—hero was—afraid to come alone,' gasped the other man.

Alex's teeth glinted in a wolf-like smile. 'The others will wait outside while you and I finish this in here.'

Marinos scrambled away, clutching himself. 'Then it is you who fight dirty. I am in big pain.'

'Are you expecting sympathy?' Alex turned on Eleanor, his eyes imperious. 'I told you to go. I need room.'

She eyed the axe. 'Are you going to kill him?'

He shrugged and turned eyes like shards of black ice on Marinos. 'You caused harm to my mother and my guest,' he said in English for Eleanor's benefit. 'Did you really expect to leave my island unpunished?'

'It was not my plan to hurt your mother.' The man glared malevolently. 'She was just best way to hurt *you*.'

'You were right. But you also enraged my father.' Marinos' face paled even more at the mention of Milo Drakos as Alex thrust out the axe and prodded him against the rough stone of the wall with its handle. 'My guest spoiled your plan, *ne*? So you hurt her. And now you pay.'

Marinos swallowed, eyes riveted on the axe blade.

Alex eyed him dispassionately. 'You paid someone to kidnap my mother, dressed up in a mask to frighten Miss Markham and then tied her up and dragged her down here, even struck her. I salute you, Paul Marinos. If I had a laurel wreath, I would crown you.'

'He wasn't the one in the mask,' Eleanor felt compelled to say. 'He doesn't do his own dirty work. He paid someone to frighten me.'

'I know. Markos went crying to Theo to confess.' Alex glared at Paul with utter contempt then turned on Eleanor. 'Go outside. Now.'

She went, outside into the dark passageway. She held up her hands to Theo, who was waiting there with Yannis. '*Parakalo, kyrie* Lazarides.'

He exclaimed in concern and took a knife to her bonds, then handed her the bracelet and gave instructions to the excited boy. 'Yannis will take you to Sofia, *kyria*.'

Holding a large torch aloft, Yannis carefully guided a very tired Eleanor through the warren of passageways up to the hall, where Sofia was waiting anxiously. He gave a hurried explanation which brought loud exclamations of horror from his mother, but as she folded Eleanor in her arms Yannis raced away, eager to return to the excitement below.

Eleanor's grasp of Greek was less than usual as she tried to assure Sofia there was nothing much wrong with her, a statement the woman dismissed with scorn. Sofia led her into the kitchen to apply a bag of ice to the bruised jaw, and smeared something soothing on the chafed wrists, all the time heaping dramatic curses on the criminal who had injured the *kyria*, and on Markos Kosta, who had helped him.

'Now you bathe, and I will bring tea.' She sighed. 'You will be glad to leave us.'

Eleanor shook her head sadly.

Sofia patted her hand. 'I will take you up to your room so you can be clean and beautiful again.'

Eleanor smiled wryly. Clean was easy; beautiful would take longer. Limp with reaction, she was glad of Sofia's company as the woman ran a hot bath, poured bath essence into it and gave orders to lie in it and relax. She offered to stay during the process, but Eleanor declined gracefully, and Sofia hurried off, as eager as her son to get back to the excitement.

The hot water was soothing on Eleanor's various bruises and scrapes, but it was hard to relax while she fretted about what was going on in the depths of the *Kastro*. Not that she had any doubts about Alex's mastery over Paul Marinos. She was also pretty sure there wouldn't be much pounding on an opponent who was not only physically inferior to him but who was suffering in the part of him that men value most. On the other hand, she could perfectly understand—and share—Alex's determination to punish the man who'd frightened Talia.

To pass the time, Eleanor put in some determined work on her appearance, but it seemed like hours before she finally heard the lift. She shot out of her room and ran along the hall into Alex's arms.

'I'm sorry I took so long. I had something to do after I finished with Paul. I didn't chop him in pieces,' he assured her huskily, 'Though I wanted to. I just smacked him around a little.' He grinned suddenly. 'I think you hurt him far more than I did, *glykia mou*.'

Her eyes flashed. 'Good. So where is he now?'

'I was tempted to leave him where he was, with the stone in place and guards outside,' Alex informed her grimly. 'But, because he is Arianna's brother, I told Theo to take Paul to the bathroom the security men use and afterwards lock him up in the exercise room.' His mouth twisted in disgust. 'Theo even persuaded me to let the man have coffee and brandy.'

Eleanor nodded in approval. 'He needs to be in some kind of shape for tomorrow. He looked pretty sick when you mentioned your father.'

'As well he might,' agreed Alex with relish. His eyes blazed as the late sun highlighted the bruise on Eleanor's jaw. 'But now I see your face, I regret leaving him conscious, *kardia mou*.' When they reached his room he picked her up and sat down with her in the chair, cradling her against him. 'Is that really all he did to you?'

She showed him her wrists. 'These are a bit sore, my shoulders too because he tied my hands behind my back—and he gagged me, which was seriously unpleasant. But I managed to hurt him before he hurt me.'

'He is very fortunate that you did, otherwise I would have taken him apart,' he said with quiet violence. 'As it is, I will leave him to Dion.'

Eleanor frowned. 'Will Dion's punishment be physical?'

Alex shook his head. 'He has little love for Paul, but he will not distress Arianna that much right now. A verbal lashing will be enough. One thing is certain—Paul Marinos will not rest easy tonight.' He held her closer, rubbing his cheek against her hair. 'Not only will he be apprehensive about the morning, he will envy me the privilege of holding you in my arms all night.'

'I don't think so, Alex.'

He held her away from him. 'You don't want to sleep with me?'

'Of course I do! But I doubt that Paul Marinos will be envious. His taste runs more to the voluptuous—like the charms of his accomplice.' She hesitated. 'Did Paul tell you about Christina?'

Alex's lip curled. 'That is why I took so long to come to you. I had to go over to Karpyros for a little talk with her about aiding and abetting Paul in his revenge. He still hates me because Christina Mavros wanted me instead of him all those years ago.' His lip curled in distaste. 'For a while after Arianna married Dion, I was fool enough to console myself with her.'

'No wonder Paul hates your guts. But so, obviously, does Christina. How long were you together?'

Alex looked uncomfortable. 'For a couple of weeks only. She wanted marriage. I did not.'

'Ah!' Eleanor shook her head. 'You Greeks are a vengeful bunch. She told those lies to a reporter to get back at you. And then she colluded with Paul over his kidnap plans for the same reason. I doubt that he'd have hurt your mother, but I fancy he would have enjoyed hurting me.'

Alex crushed her close. 'If he had succeeded he would not be drinking my brandy right now, *kardia mou.*'

'He didn't succeed. I learned a bit of basic self-defence in college and got in first. I hear Sofia coming by the way,' she said into his chest.

'Then I will have a bath while you drink your tea.' He smiled as he stood her on her feet. 'But just tea, *parakolo*, because I asked Sofia to serve dinner very early tonight.'

Eleanor's face heated as she made for the door. 'What reason did you give?'

'None,' he said, surprised, with the typical hubris which half-irritated, half-delighted her.

Alex watched her go, a smile playing about his lips, and then made for the bathroom to stand under water as hot as he could bear. He needed purifying heat after the encounter with Paul Marinos, who had grown from an indulged, petulant teenager into a bored, discontented man who found a fitting partner in crime in Christina Mavros. She would have been only too delighted to help him hurt Alexei Drakos.

He smiled as he thought of her face when he found her waiting for Paul in a *taverna* on Karpyros. It had been a great pleasure to inform her that Paul's plan had gone badly wrong, and if she were wise she'd get the hell out of Karpyros and never show her face there again. And this time, he'd made it clear, there were to be no more colourful lies to the press. Otherwise Alexei would publish the facts about her involvement in kidnap and blackmail with Paul Marinos. There'd been furious protestations of innocence, but in the end Christina had taken the next ferry home to Crete. Alex's mouth curled in disgust at the thought of Paul Marinos. Deprived of his knife, the clever swine had put up no fight against fists which had battered him in furious retaliation for the way he'd treated Eleanor. Paul had known that putting up no defence was the only way to cut short his punishment.

Alex's towelled off in a hurry, thrust his fingers through his hair by way of grooming and then anointed his sore knuckles with some of Sofia's special balm. He pulled on a white T-shirt and jeans soft with age, his mind occupied with ways to make his last night with Eleanor one she would look back on with such pleasure she would want to repeat it very soon. His eyes glinted. He would bring his trip to London forward with just that aim in mind.

Sofia was laying the table when Eleanor reached the tower room. 'I brought tea for you, *kyria*,' she said and smiled in approval. 'You look better now.'

'I feel better.' Eleanor cast an eye over the dish of pastries on the tray. 'These look gorgeous.'

'I made *kyrie* Alexei's favourites.' She gave Eleanor a woman-to-woman smile. 'He asked me to serve dinner early, which is good. You need a good sleep ready for your journey tomorrow.'

'Thank you, Sofia.'

The woman laid a hand on Eleanor's as she turned to go. 'I am ashamed that a friend of Yannis should harm you, *kyria*. Markos is not a bad boy. His parents died when he was young, and he lives with a sister who has a large family. Life is not easy for him. To earn such money for so little was too much temptation.' She rolled her large dark eyes. 'Also it was big fun to wear that stupid mask—but he did not mean to make you faint, *kyria*.'

Having understood most of this, Eleanor patted Sofia's hand. 'I understand.'

'You are a kind young lady. I am sad to see you go. Come back soon.'

Eleanor smiled, her throat too tight to answer, and with a sigh poured some tea, depressed. But when Alex came to join her the sight and scent of him pushed aside all thoughts of leaving to concentrate on the heady pleasure of now.

Sofia served grilled swordfish, and a dish of *keftedes*, the pork meatballs Eleanor had enjoyed in several eating places during her island-hopping. 'Just for you, *kyrie*,' Sofia told Alex as she left them.

'Rustic food, but my favourite,' he commented as he seated Eleanor. 'Sofia makes them for me every time I come here.'

'I've eaten them all round the Aegean. I like those bits of pork they grill on skewers, too.' She thought for a moment. '*Souvlakia*?'

He grinned. 'You're trying to impress me, but you're a journalist, *kyria* Markham. You take notes.'

Her eyes flashed. 'And pretty nasty you were when you first saw me doing it.' She tasted her fish with pleasure. 'This is so good. I don't eat enough fish at home—at least not this kind—' She stopped, flushing. 'Why are you looking at me like that?'

Alex smiled slowly, the look in his eyes hot enough to melt her bones. 'Because I hunger for you, *glykia mou,* far more than for Sofia's excellent dinner.'

With effort she tore her eyes away. 'Eat it just the same, Alex, or Sofia will be hurt.'

'I know.' His eyes darkened. 'But it does my appetite no good to know that tomorrow you are leaving. And before I can take you to the airport I must deal with Dion and Paul.'

'You have absolutely no need to come with me to Crete,' she protested. 'I'm not in any kind of danger now.'

'I will see you onto the plane, Eleanor,' he stated with such finality she gave in.

'Alex,' she said later, giving up the struggle. 'I just can't eat any more.'

'I will ring Sofia and ask her to bring coffee and leave the pastries for us to eat later.' He smiled crookedly as he got up. 'I will even help clear the food away, ready for her.'

She smiled. 'How you've changed since we first met, *kyrie* Drakos!'

'You are such a good influence!' He rang down to the kitchen to speak to Sofia, then took Eleanor by the hand and led her to the sofa. 'Sit with me here while we wait for her.'

'When will Dion get here?'

'He has a fast boat, so he will arrive early in the morning.'

Eleanor hesitated. 'Are you on good terms with him?'

'You mean even though he stole Arianna from me?'

'I suppose I meant that, yes.'

'We are in business together with the wine, and sometimes Arianna asks me to dine with them, but from a personal point of view Dion and I will never be soul-mates. His life is centred here in his beloved islands, while mine is more global in my aim to eclipse my father.' He smiled crookedly. 'I have not succeeded in that yet, but I keep striving.'

Eleanor's hand tightened on his. 'I get the feeling you're a little less hostile to him than you were. Are you thawing towards your father?'

'To a certain extent, yes,' he admitted reluctantly. 'But at one time, when I found he doubted my paternity, I wanted to kill him. Yet I owe him in one way, because my anger made me determined to make it on my own in life without any help from him.'

'He offered help?'

'Yes.'

'But you refused it, of course.'

'Of course.' His chin rose. 'I not only had money I'd made myself, I inherited a generous legacy from my grandfather. I needed no help from my father—or from anyone else. Besides, any hope of reconciliation between us died when I found his mistress staying with him on Corfu.' His eyes darkened. 'She tried to poison me to make me go away.'

Eleanor stared at the stern, beautiful face silhouetted against the fading light. 'Is that why you were ill?'

Alex nodded. 'She was clever enough to make me just sick enough to go home and leave the field clear for her.' His face hardened. 'She need not have troubled. When I found Melania there, I couldn't get away fast enough.'

'And afterwards you shut your father out of your life,' she said softly and hesitated. 'Did your mother do the same?'

'I don't know. Mother will never talk about him.' He shrugged. 'But it must have been obvious the other night that they are not indifferent to each other. Nor,' he added darkly, 'Do I think it was the only time they'd seen each other recently.'

'It seemed obvious to me that he cares for you too, Alex.'

'Only because he has no other son to carry on his name.' He smiled as Sofia came in with a tray. He spoke to her at length and she nodded and patted his hand, then came to Eleanor and patted hers.

'You were too sad to leave to eat much tonight,' she said slowly so Eleanor could understand. She turned to Alex. 'Do I give the prisoner food?'

'Yes. But *kyrie* Lazarides must take it to him, not Yannis,' he ordered, and she nodded and wished them goodnight.

Alex drew Eleanor to her feet. 'And now,' he said, kissing her hand, 'I think we should take this tray to our room and lock the world away, *ne*?'

'Oh yes,' she sighed, and smiled as she saw that Sofia had provided both tea and coffee. 'I'll miss all this when I get home.'

'Will you miss me, too?'

'Yes,' she said baldly as he hurried her along to his room.

Alex stood aside to let Eleanor through, then

carried the tray to his dressing chest and turned back to lock the door. 'Is that true?' he demanded, drawing her to him.

'Of course it is. My life will be dull at home after all the excitement here.' She smiled ruefully. 'I had such a great time exploring the Greek islands for my travel series, yet I can't write about even half of the things that have happened to me on yours or you'll sue the paper and I'll lose my job.'

He shook his head. 'I will not be forced to sue, *kyria* journalist, because I trust you.'

'Thank you, *kyrie* Drakos. I'm honoured.'

'*You* should be. I trust very few people in this world.' He picked her up and placed her on the bed against the stacked pillows. '*You* have been subjected to such trauma today, I will personally serve you tea and pastries.' His eyes glinted. 'Another reason for you to feel unique. I do this for no one else.'

'Not even your mother?'

He shook his head. 'In England my mother has a housekeeper whose sole aim in life is to ensure her comfort—physical and mental. Grace is the ex-policewoman who left Mother to get married, but the marriage was short-lived. When my grandfather died, Mother decided to make England her permanent home and asked Grace to join her.' He handed Eleanor a cup of tea. 'She is not only intelligent and loyal but also a crack shot. Talia Kazan is in safe hands.' He filled his coffee cup and sat down in the big bedside chair, frowning at Eleanor. 'I wish you had someone like Grace in your life.'

She grinned. 'I don't need ordinary household help for my place, let alone a crack-shot ex-policewoman!'

Alex put their empty cups on the tray and sat on the edge of the bed, tracing a finger over the bruise on her jaw. 'When I came back to find you missing, I thought you'd persuaded someone to take you over to Karpyros to catch the ferry to Crete.'

She stared up at him blankly. 'Why on earth would I do that?'

He shrugged. 'To find you gone was so bad a shock I wasn't thinking straight. Then I looked in your room and saw nothing had been taken, and questioned Sofia, at which point Theo came rushing to say Markos had confessed his sins—

so we knew where to look for you, even without the clue of your bracelet.'

'With no handy ball of string to unwind, or crumbs or pebbles to trail like Hansel and Gretel, it was the only thing I could think of to leave as a clue. My hands were tied behind me, so I managed to work the fastening open without Paul noticing in his tearing rush to get me down the stairs. It's only by good luck I got to that nasty little hidey-hole in one piece.' Eleanor smiled at him. 'But I knew you'd come for me.'

'I would have torn the place apart!' Alex drew her into his arms and held her close.

Somewhere in the back of her mind, the part that wasn't fully engaged with the sheer pleasure of contact, Eleanor was surprised. She had expected Alex to make love to her the moment they were alone, yet he seemed happy just to hold her and talk.

'What are you thinking?' His warm breath against her cheek almost made her purr.

'That it's good just to lie here like this with you and talk.'

He raised his head to smile at her. 'The other

men in your life consider talk a waste of valuable time in this situation?'

Eleanor thought it over. 'There is absolutely no one in my life I could picture in this particular situation. The only men interested in actually talking to me are colleagues.'

'I take great pleasure in your conversation.' He kissed her fleetingly. 'This period on Kyrkiros has not been peaceful for *you*, Eleanor, but I will look back on it as a halcyon time when I was granted the privilege of your company.'

'That's such a lovely thing to say,' she said huskily.

'It's the simple truth.' His eyes were abruptly searching. 'Paul subjected you to a very bad experience today. Are you fully recovered?'

'No, I'm not.' Her eyes lit with a smile which tightened his embrace. 'I'm in desperate need of someone to guard me against nightmares.'

He laughed deep in his throat. 'You have him, right here in the hollow of your hand, *agape mou*.'

'How lovely!' She kissed him so ardently heat flared in his eyes, igniting a response which shot fire through her body down to her toes. 'But if you want to stop talking for a while now, it's fine by me, Alex.'

His breathing quickened. 'Are you asking me to make love to you?'

'Do I have to ask?'

'*Ochi*!' He kissed her with a hunger she responded to with such abandon he undressed her rapidly, managing to render her naked without taking his mouth from hers.

'Very clever! You've done that before,' she gasped when he stood up to take off his clothes.

Alex gave her a smile which took away what little breath she had left. 'I have,' he admitted, and returned to his place in her embrace. 'But with you it is not skill, but reluctance to stop kissing you even to—' He broke off with a smothered curse as his phone rang. With a swift apology, he listened intently and then began a conversation in Greek so fluent and rapid she couldn't understand a word of it. At last Alex closed the phone and stretched out to put it on the bedside table, then took her in his arms and rubbed his cheek against hers.

'Bad news?' she asked after a while.

'No, it was very good news.' He raised his head,

smiling down at her wryly. 'Arianna has just presented Dion with a second son. He regrets that due to this he cannot come from Crete in person to collect Paul as promised. To avoid any distress for Arianna, he will send some of his men to take our prisoner to Naros. Dion begged me to tell her nothing about her brother's behaviour until she is recovered from the birth.'

'I should think not!' Eleanor eyed him with sympathy. 'Are you a little bit jealous? It would be only natural if you were. Arianna was yours before she married Dion.'

Alex shook his head. 'Arianna was never mine in the way you mean. We were loving friends at one time, and still are. But her relationship with Dion is different. He worships her.'

'Does she reciprocate?'

He smiled crookedly. 'As I told you before, once she met Dion she had eyes for no one else.'

Eleanor knew the feeling. One look at Alexei and she had fallen head over heels in love. Otherwise she wouldn't be here in his arms, taking full advantage of every fleeting moment until she flew home and crash-landed back to earth.

'What are you thinking?' whispered Alex, smoothing a caressing hand down her spine.

'I'm counting, not thinking.'

'This is a time for mathematics?' He chuckled and kissed her nose. 'What are you counting, *kardia mou*?'

'The minutes left before I go.'

'Stop!' he commanded, his face stern as his arms closed round her. 'I know you must leave tomorrow, but it does not mean goodbye. I will come to you in England very soon.'

'Let's not talk about it now,' she pleaded. 'We're wasting those minutes I mentioned.'

'I thought you liked men to talk to you!'

'I do. But right now, Alexei Drakos, I want you to—'

He smothered the rest of her sentence with a kiss which made it clear that, whatever she wanted, he wanted it even more. His mouth roved her face, gentle as it reached her bruised jaw.

'I could kill him just for this,' he growled against her parted lips.

'Never mind him,' she ordered fiercely. 'Just kiss it better. And then move on down to my other bruises too. If you like.'

He gave a delighted laugh and did as she commanded, then raised his head to look into her eyes. 'To make sure no bruises are left unattended, I must kiss you all over.'

'Lovely! Have you got any bruises in need of attention? Or shall I just kiss you all over too?' She bent her head to begin with his chest, teasing him with the tip of her tongue in open-mouthed kisses that tensed every muscle in his body.

Alex drew in a deep, shuddering breath. 'This is hard to endure.'

'Endure? You don't like it?'

'I like it so much I am ready to explode.' And with a swift move, he rolled her on her back and held himself poised above her. 'Eleanor, are you sure you want me this way tonight?'

She stared up at him in astonishment. 'How clear must I be? You want an email in confirmation?'

He laughed unsteadily. 'I thought that after your treatment at the hands of that man you might not want to make love tonight.'

'I want to make love with *you* tonight, Alex.' In sudden desperation, she caught him in a caress that put an abrupt end to all verbal communication. Their bodies joined together in such immediate urgency their loving was savagely short, but so sweet they remained entwined as they came slowly back to earth, his arms possessive around her, his bright curls tangled with her dark, tumbled hair as they lay cheek to cheek.

Alex stirred a little and kissed her. 'Are you thirsty, *kardia mou?*'

'Yes. But I don't want you to move. Stay just as you are a little longer, *parakolo.* Or even a lot longer,' she added shamelessly.

He chuckled. 'As long as you wish. Though there is risk like this, you understand.'

'I do.' She gave him a smile as old as Eve as she felt him harden and kissed him to show her appreciation.

Alex's response was immediate and impassioned, his mouth possessive as his hands moved over her in caresses that slowly turned her entire body into an entire throbbing erogenous zone. She gasped, her fingers caressing his back, delighting in the strength of his long, flat muscles as he began to move, urging her with him, slowly at first, then gradually faster in breathless, heart-pounding rhythm on the quest for completion which overtook her before him. He held her tightly as she gasped in the throes of her climax, and with super-human control waited until she relaxed before surrendering to the overwhelming pleasure of his own.

Later, Eleanor lay awake in Alex's arms, determined to savour every moment of the swiftly passing night. She could sleep when she got home. Tonight she would drain every last drop of pleasure from this once in a lifetime experience.

'You must be tired, *glykia mou*,' said Alex in her ear. 'Can you not sleep?'

'Am I disturbing you?'

'No.' He pulled her closer. 'This bed will seem very empty next time I sleep in it, though God knows when that will be.'

'Where will you go after I'm gone?'

'To Athens first. Stefan is growing very insistent. Will you go straight back to work, Eleanor?'

'I'll spend a day or so with my parents, then get back to my desk to polish my series up, ready to meet my deadline—and afterwards do whatever comes next.' A yawn overtook her and Alex chuckled as he held her closer.

'You need sleep, *kardia mou*.'

Eleanor knew it and, though she struggled to keep awake, the events of the day, followed by the passionate love-making of the night, finally conquered her as she fell deeply asleep in the security of Alexei Drakos' embrace.

CHAPTER TEN

ELEANOR woke late next morning to the scent of coffee and found Alex, bright-eyed and damp of hair, smiling down at her as he offered her a cup.

'*Kalimera*, sleepy-head.'

'Good morning.' She struggled upright and pushed the hair out of her eyes, wishing he'd given her time to look at least human. 'I didn't hear you in the shower.'

'I stole out for a swim so I wouldn't wake you.' He sat on the edge of the bed, watching her drink. 'How are you this morning, *glykia mou*?'

'Half-asleep.' She drained the last of the coffee and felt the caffeine start to take effect. 'I'm not a morning person.'

'So I see.' He took the cup from her and threw the covers back, laughing as her eyes sparked at him like an angry cat's. 'I brought my mother's robe, so you can shower here, ready for the breakfast Sofia will bring to the tower room in fifteen minutes.'

She shook her head as she wrapped herself in the robe to collect her discarded clothes. 'I'll just sprint along to my bathroom, thanks just the same. See you in ten.'

Alex tried to change her mind by underhanded means but she laughed and dodged away to run along the hall, determined to look as presentable as possible for their last breakfast together. After the fastest shower on record she tied her damp hair up in a pony-tail rather than attempt to dry it. In jeans and T-shirt, ready to travel, she slapped moisturiser on her glowing face, added a lick of lip gloss and made it to the tower room seconds before Sofia appeared with their breakfast.

'You were very fast, Eleanor,' said Alex, holding her chair for her.

'Years of practice,' she assured him. 'Though I don't eat a breakfast like this every day.'

'You should,' he said, looking oddly tense as he sat down. 'Does your housemate leave early also?'

'Yes. Pat is usually out of the house before me.'

'You get on well together?'

'Very well. We've known each other for years.'

Eleanor looked at him anxiously. 'Have you seen Paul this morning?'

Alex nodded briefly. 'He looked ready to murder Christina when I told him she had left him to face the music alone.'

'When are Dion's men arriving to collect him?'

'He rang me while you were dressing. They are on their way. Arianna and the new baby are doing well, he reported.' Alex met her eyes. 'But someone else is arriving first, Eleanor—my father wants to confront the man who caused harm to my mother.'

'Heavens!' She took in a deep breath. 'Would you prefer me to keep out of the way until he leaves?'

Alex eyed her in surprise. '*Ochi*! My father wishes to speak to you, Eleanor.'

She bit her lip. 'Does he know I'm a journalist? If so please tell him I have no intention of writing about him.'

Alex gave a short, mirthless laugh. 'Milo Drakis would not care a damn if you did. But he would care very much if you wrote about my mother.' His eyes softened. 'But I have your word that you will not.'

Eleanor downed her coffee and stood up. 'Yes,' she said with emphasis. 'You have. I must go and pack. I'll be in my room if you want me.'

Alex got to his feet, frowning. 'Why not stay here with me?'

'I need to get my belongings together, send off a few emails and so on,' she said, evading his eyes.

'As you wish—' Alex broke off to answer his phone, then closed it and smiled wryly. 'My father is at the jetty. He is early.'

'I'll get out of your way, then,' Eleanor said hastily and made for the door, but Alex caught her before she reached it and swept her into his arms to kiss her.

'I will come for you later,' he promised and retained her hand as they hurried along the hall to the lift. He raised her hand to his lips then went inside, his eyes holding hers until the lift doors closed on him.

After nearly three weeks of constant travelling, Eleanor had packing down to a fine art. Once her clothes were put away she tucked her camera in her battered tote bag with her travel documents and wallet and a couple of paperbacks, her mind on what was happening down below with

Paul Marinos. She checked that nothing was left in the bathroom and then took a last look round the room, suddenly so impatient to get the pain of departure over with, it was a relief to hear the expected knock on her door.

'My father is waiting,' Alex informed her. 'He would like to see you before he leaves.'

'What happened with Paul?' she asked as they made for the tower room.

'When he saw my father he was all grovelling apologies, but insisted that Christina should share the blame,' said Alex with disgust, and stood back for her to enter the tower room, where the imposing figure of Milo Drakos stood at the windows, gazing out at the view.

He turned as they entered and took Eleanor's hand to bow over it. 'I am glad of this opportunity to thank you for your brave help to my wife, Ms Markham—also to express my deep regrets for the hurt you suffered at the hands of Paul Marinos.'

'I'm fine now, except for a few bruises,' she assured him.

He smiled at her warmly, and looked at Alex,

eyebrows raised. 'The man is not short of money, so revenge on you was obviously his sole motive.'

'And he didn't care who suffered in the process of achieving it,' agreed Alex harshly. 'He's lucky I didn't kill him yesterday.'

'I am grateful you did not,' said Milo Drakos dryly. 'I would have objected to seeing my son imprisoned—Marinos is not worth paying such a price.'

'And, even worse, I would have earned Arianna's wrath,' said Alex wryly. 'He's her brother, and blood is blood.'

'What will happen to him now?' asked Eleanor.

'I have discussed this with my son,' said Milo. 'Alexei is hot to see Marinos imprisoned for his intentions towards my wife, and the hurt he inflicted on you, Miss Markham—'

'He *struck* Eleanor, Father, and so did the man he hired to kidnap my mother!' broke in Alex. 'Eleanor has many more bruises than the one visible on her face.'

'You are embarrassing her, but I am in complete sympathy with you, Alexei, since your mother suffered bruises also,' observed Milo as Eleanor's face crimsoned. 'However, since you inflicted far more on Paul Marinos—relieved him of two teeth, and his nose will never recover its shape—you have exacted *your* revenge, *ne*?'

'Not enough,' said Alex harshly.

His father turned to Eleanor. 'To avoid publicity to my family, Ms Markham, and because Arianna Aristides has just given birth, I will not have her brother changed with the crimes he intended to commit against my family, because he was ultimately prevented from committing them. You, however, are at liberty to have charged him with bodily harm and attempted abduction.'

Eleanor shook her head. 'I'm about to leave for the UK, Mr Drakos. I'd rather forget about the whole thing.'

'And will you write about your adventure?' he said gently.

She looked him in the eye. 'No. I've given my word to Alexei that I won't mention your wife, nor what happened to me here. I will, of course, give a glowing account of the festival and the idyllic life *other* people lead here on Kyrkiros.'

Milo Drakos smiled and raised her hand to his lips. 'It has been a great privilege to meet you,

Miss Markham. I hope we meet again in pleas-anter circumstances.'

'It's kind of you to say so, but I doubt it.' Elea-nor exchanged a look with Alex. 'This kind of experience doesn't happen twice.'

'I will leave it to Alexei to change your mind,' said Milo, eyes gleaming.

Alex closed his phone. 'Dion's men are here, Father. It's time to throw Paul Marinos off my island.'

Milo Drakos bowed over Eleanor's hand. 'Good-bye, my dear.'

She smiled. 'Goodbye, Mr Drakos.'

'Once Paul has gone, I'll see my father off, El-eanor,' said Alex. 'Wait for me here—*parakolo*,' he added at a look from his parent.

Eleanor went back to her room to look from her windows at the beach below and watched as Milo Drakos talked at length to his son and then of-fered him his hand. *Take it,* she said silently and, as though he'd heard her, Alex not only grasped the hand but even received the kiss his father be-stowed on his cheek. Eleanor turned away rather than intrude, even from this distance, on some-thing so intensely private. When Alex eventually joined her in the tower room, she was presiding over the coffee tray Sofia had sent up with Yannis.

'So Paul is on his way, Alex.'

'Not yet.' He turned to her, a wry look in his eyes. 'You're not going to believe this. Before he left, my father asked for my blessing. He wants to marry my mother again.'

Eleanor gazed at him, wide-eyed. 'What on earth did you say?'

'I told him it was her blessing he needed, not mine.' Alex shook his head in disbelief. 'What the hell was I supposed to say? In the end I assured my father that if she is happy about it, I won't raise any objections.' He smiled crookedly. 'He was pleased.'

From the tableau she'd witnessed Eleanor, could well believe it. 'I hope it works out for them. And for you.' She disengaged herself to pour coffee. 'I'm sorry to introduce a more mundane subject, but I must leave after lunch to catch the ferry.'

'You could leave a lot later if we went by helicopter—' He broke off as his phone rang. '*Me synchoreite*—I must answer this.'

Eleanor gazed out at the view as Alex spoke to

the caller with increasing urgency, then closed his phone, his face grim.

'That was Dion again, asking for my help. He wants me to follow his men over to Naros to make sure Paul gets there. Once he is sure all is well with Arianna, he will arrive there later today himself—but in the meantime he wants to make sure little brother doesn't feed some sob story to his captors and persuade them to take him home to Crete to upset his sister.'

'Would they do that?'

'The men have known him all his life, and because his face is a mess right now they might.' Alex sighed and ran a hand through his hair. 'If you wait to go by helicopter, I can be back in time to fly you to Crete. But, if I can't make it in time, simply stay another night.' He took her in his arms, rubbing his cheek against hers. 'In fact, *kyria*, that is a very good idea, *ne?*'

'A brilliant idea.' Eleanor smiled at him and gave him a little push as he drew her to her feet. 'In the meantime, go and evict Paul Marinos from your island, *kyrie* Drakos.'

CHAPTER ELEVEN

ELEANOR stood at the window again, watching as Paul Marinos limped to the jetty between two men who helped him into a boat while Alex boarded his own. She watched both crafts roaring away across the sea then went to her room and sat down at the dressing table, to gaze into space for a while before drafting a note which took several attempts before she finally sealed it in an envelope.

This has been a wonderful, magical experience, Alex. But, rather than spoil the magic by trying to prolong it, we must both return to the real world. Since fate has stepped in to take you off with Paul, I'll ask Yannis to get me to Karpyros to catch the ferry. Please don't be angry with me. Thank you again for the interview.
Eleanor.

She knuckled tears from her eyes, wrote Alex's name on the envelope, then switched off her phone, collected her bags and carried them along to the lift to take down to the hall. Sofia objected strongly when she heard the *kyria* was leaving alone, but Eleanor explained why, as best as she could, and handed over the letter.

'Give this to *kyrie* Alexei, please. Can Yannis take me over to Karpyros right away?' she asked, suddenly so miserably unhappy, Sofia took her in her arms to pat her back soothingly before she went outside to call to her son.

Eleanor's relief was intense when the plane took off on time from Crete. Normally she was uptight at take-off until the plane reached its altitude. But after a wait at the airport, wound tight as a coiled spring in case a furious Alex appeared at any moment, she leaned back in her seat as the plane began its climb, and finally began to relax. In spite of guilt about stealing away, she was utterly certain it was the right thing to do. She'd meant every word about her magical stay on Kyrkiros but, much as she would have liked to stay another day—and night—it was time to leave. Enchantment on an island in the sun was an experience she was passionately grateful for, but only a romantic fool would expect it to survive a transfer to the reality of daily life on her home ground.

Not that Alex was likely to track her down there. Instead of working in London for one of the major newspapers, as he probably believed, her job was actually on the features section of a provincial paper in a town a long way from the capital. She loved the town, and she enjoyed her job, but a hotshot journalist she was not. At least, not yet. Her aim had always been a post with a major London broadsheet, so as a step towards it her interview with Alexei Drakos would do wonders for her CV. She blinked hard. Lord knew, she'd earned it.

Eleanor's parents were waiting for her at Birmingham airport to drive her to their retirement cottage near Cirencester. After the high drama of her stay on Kyrkiros, it was restful to do nothing much at all for the entire time she spent there, other than give descriptions of all the islands she'd visited, eat her mother's cooking and deal with the laundry she insisted on doing herself. Jane Markham was deeply impressed by Eleanor's account of Talia Kazan and studied the photographs in wonder.

'She's hardly changed at all! Fancy you meeting her by chance. What's she like?'

Eleanor was able to say, with perfect truth, that Talia Kazan's personality was as lovely as her face. 'An absolute charmer. She even managed to persuade her son to give me the interview Ross wanted.'

'I read the article in the paper,' said her father in approval. 'McLean got it in pretty sharpish— I've kept it for you to see. This Alexei Drakos is a striking chap, from his photograph.'

'Is he a charmer too?' asked Jane, smiling.

'Not quite the way I'd describe him, no, Mother. Too strong a personality.'

George Markham shot a look at her. 'You didn't like him?'

'Actually, I liked him very much.' This was such a lukewarm description of her feelings, she changed the subject by asking to see the paper, and found not only Alexei's photograph above the article but her own face in miniature under the heading.

* * *

Eleanor arrived back at her desk at the *Chronicle* to an immediate summons from Ross McLean.

'Thanks a lot, Markham!' He brandished a London tabloid in front of her and jabbed a finger at the gossip column. 'Explain this.'

To her horror Eleanor saw current photographs of Talia Kazan and Milo Drakos topping a piece headed:

ESTRANGED COUPLE REUNITED?

Talia Kazan, iconic supermodel of yesteryear, who divorced property tycoon Milo Drakos a year after she married him, has been spotted on the Aegean island owned by Alexei Drakos, their entrepreneur son. Since Milo was on hand too, maybe there's a reunion on the cards for the Greek Goddess and the Tycoon! How will Alexei, allegedly hostile to his father, feel about that?

'Well?' demanded Ross. 'You were there, so you must have seen Talia Kazan. The article you wrote was dull stuff compared to this. Did you sell the information to this rag?'

'I most certainly did not.' Eleanor's eyes flashed angrily. 'The only way I could get the "dull stuff" you were so delighted about was to promise Alexei Drakos I would make no mention of his mother.'

'So who the hell wrote this?'

'No idea. There was a festival on the island with crowds of people. Anyone could have seen Talia Kazan and Milo Drakos, though they were never together in public.'

'But you must have seen them!'

'I met Ms Kazan, who invited me to sit with her party at the festival. In fact,' she added fiercely, 'She was the one who persuaded her son to give me the interview. He agreed on condition I made no mention of her, but if they read this rubbish they'll think I broke my word.'

Calmer now, Ross eyed her speculatively. 'Which matters a lot to you.'

More than he could possibly know. 'Alexei Drakos said he'd sue the paper if his mother's name appeared, which is quite funny if you think of it!'

'Hilarious,' agreed Ross, looking happier. 'He can sue this tabloid as much as he likes. He gave me precise instructions before he would give the go-ahead on the article, not least that charming portrait of you to go with it. I've sold the piece on, of course so, when you leave me one day for the metropolis, as I know damn well you intend, your face will be familiar to the London big boys.'

She sniffed. 'You've never given me the honour before.'

'I complied with Drakos' demands. He expresses himself pretty forcibly, even by email. Good-looking bloke.' Ross showed his veneers in a sly smile. 'Did you like him?'

'Yes, I did,' said Eleanor briefly. 'So, now you know I didn't turn Judas on you, boss, when do you want the first of my travel articles?'

'Today, of course.'

'Of course.'

'With the photographs for the entire series.'

'Right.'

Eleanor was glad to get busy, but felt as though a thick black cloud hung over her desk as she worked. She was only too pleased to get away from it for lunch with fellow female journalists, who praised her for the interview with Alexei Drakos, and commiserated about the tabloid article. Back at her desk, she got the first of her Greek travel articles out on deadline with the accompanying photographs, and worked hard on the rest. Ross had decided to feature them all week, with the Kyrkiros feature in the Saturday magazine as the finale, courtesy of the shots of the bull dance, which even Ross had to admit were fairly good.

'Fairly good?' snorted Sandra Morris, the health columnist. 'They're brilliant, El. You surpassed yourself.'

'Good light in the Greek islands.'

'Oh, come on, the dancers were shot by torch-light, by the look of it. What's up? You haven't been yourself since you got back.'

'I'm a bit tired.' And the role of Damocles was a strain. She kept waiting for the sword to fall on her neck.

By the end of the day, Eleanor persuaded herself that the tabloid article had probably slipped under the radar where Alex and his family were concerned. Talia was unlikely to buy the a tabloid, and since Alex and Milo were in Greece they probably wouldn't have seen it either. Lord, she hoped not! When she got home to a warm welcome from Pat Mellor, they ate supper together and regaled each other with news of their respective holidays. Life, Eleanor felt, could now get back to normal, except for thoughts of Alex that kept her awake at night. And not just thoughts. To Eleanor's utter dismay, her body yearned for the physical bliss of their love-making.

Mike Denny, cricket correspondent, gave her a nudge as he passed her desk next day.

'Your presence is required, El.'

Eleanor looked up to see Ross beckoning from his office door, a look on his face which boded ill for someone; obviously her. She got up and joined him, smiling in polite enquiry

'You wanted me?'

'Shut the door,' he snapped and sat down behind his desk. 'Sit down.'

Ross McLean rarely invited reporters to sit unless he was firing them. Eleanor sat, resigned, waiting for the sword to fall.

'This came from Alexei Drakos just now. Instead of shooting it to your inbox, I printed it.' He pushed a sheet of paper across the desk.

I need Eleanor Markham's telephone number and home address immediately.

'He's obviously read the tabloid article,' said Eleanor when she could trust her voice.

'He doesn't say so. Imperious blighter, isn't he? Well?' added Ross. 'Do I do as he wants?'

'Not much choice, I suppose.' She sighed, depressed. 'Only make sure it's my address here in Pennington. I don't want him descending on my parents like a wolf on the fold.'

'Right. Whatever you say.' Ross eyed her with unusual kindness. 'Better make sure you're not alone when he calls to see you.'

'He won't come to *see* me. He'll just blister my ears via the phone.'

'Because he's contacted the tabloid by now and found you don't work there?'

She nodded miserably. 'I sort of gave the impression that I'm based in London, so he's going to be pretty furious when he finds I'm not.'

'What exactly *were* you up to on your trip, Markham?' he demanded. 'Anything I should know about if he comes rampaging in here?'

'I was doing the work I'm paid for,' she said flatly, and got up. 'Talking of which, I'd better get on.'

Ross got to his feet, his sharp-featured face

deadly serious. 'Look, if you need back-up of any kind just shout, Eleanor. The *Chronicle* looks after its employees, so refer Drakos to me if he cuts up rough.'

She smiled, touched. 'Thank you.'

Eleanor got home late that night after hustling to meet her deadline, exhausted by the tension of expecting a phone call from Alex any minute. When Pat called as she was on her way upstairs, she was in no mood to chat.

'Hold it, El.'

She turned, forcing a smile. 'What's up?'

'I should be asking you that! You had a visitor an hour ago; a forceful gentleman who wanted to punch my lights out when I said lived here—with you.' Pat grinned. 'Had you deceived him, old thing? Told him I was a girl?'

'Sorry to puncture your ego, Mellor, but I didn't talk about you at all,' Eleanor snapped, and sat down suddenly on one of the stairs. 'What happened?'

Pat leapt up to sit beside her. 'He ordered me to tell you he will be back. Sort of like The Terminator, only *much* better looking.'

Eleanor groaned, and leaned against Pat's broad shoulder. 'He wasn't brandishing a newspaper, by any chance?'

'No. I recognised him, though. He's the Greek bloke you interviewed on your odyssey. I read the article. Did you sell your body to get the scoop or something? By the look of him it would have been no sacrifice— Oh God, El, I was joking! Don't *cry*!' Pat pulled her close and stroked her hair while she drenched his shirt with the first tears she'd shed since returning home.

After a while Pat pulled her to her feet and took her down to his kitchen. He sat her on a stool at the bar and mopped her face with kitchen towel before filling the kettle.

'Coffee, tea or whisky?'

'Better make it hemlock,' she said thickly and scrubbed at her eyes.

'No need to go overboard with the Greek thing, pet! You'll settle for a nice cup of tea while you tell Uncle Pat all about it.'

Eleanor gave the bare bones of her tale as succinctly as possible, and even managed a laugh with Pat when it came to Alexei Drakos in possible litigation with the tabloid.

'I bet your revered editor liked that bit! Though Drakos couldn't do that, could he? Was there any libel in the article?'

'No. Just speculation, really. Someone spotted Talia Kazan and her ex-husband on the island during the festival and sold the information to the highest bidder—which just happened to be the tabloid that's an infamous purveyor of celebrity gossip. Alex will never believe I'm not the culprit,' said Eleanor despondently.

'"Alex"?' said Pat, eyebrows raised.

She ignored him and took refuge in her tea.

'Do you want something with that, love?'

'Painkillers would be good.' Eleanor gave him a watery smile. 'Hope I haven't wrecked your evening. Were you going out?'

He shook his head, grinning. 'Which is damn lucky—I might have missed all the drama!'

She eyed him apprehensively. 'When Alex said he'd be back, did he specify when?'

'No—and I wasn't brave enough to ask! But, if you want some support when he does, I'm your man.'

Eleanor chuckled and slid off the stool. 'Thanks, friend, but I'm not afraid of Alexei Drakos.'

'Good to know.' Pat was suddenly serious. 'I meant it, though.'

'I know you did.' She kissed his cheek. 'Good-night.'

For Pat's benefit, Eleanor marched upstairs like a soldier prepared for battle, but once she closed her bedroom door she leaned back against it, a hand across her eyes for a minute or two before making for the bathroom to swallow painkillers. She thought about making a meal but ran a hot bath instead. If her head hadn't ached so much, she would have screamed in frustration when her doorbell rang almost immediately and she had to get out of the bath again to answer. She snatched up the intercom receiver, knowing the identity of her visitor without asking.

'Alexei Drakos. I need to talk to you.'

'It's late.'

'It is not. Let me in,' he ordered. 'Or shall I ask your good friend Pat to do it?'

She pressed the buzzer that opened the main door, then shrugged into her dressing gown, dragged a comb through her wet hair and went out onto the landing to find Alex talking to Pat in the hall, imposing in a dark city suit. He looked up at her, one eyebrow raised.

'*Geia sas,* Eleanor.'

'Hello.' She smiled reassuringly at Pat, who looked very unhappy about leaving her alone with her visitor. 'Don't worry, I'll be fine.'

Alex scowled at him. 'You think I mean to harm her?'

Pat scowled back. 'You'd better not, mate! If you want me, just shout,' he told Eleanor.

'Come up,' she told Alex and turned to make for her sitting room, noting that it was reasonably tidy as he followed her inside. Not that she cared. 'Do sit down,' she said politely, but he shut the door and stayed standing, hot accusation in his eyes.

'You ran away!'

She nodded dumbly.

'Why?'

'Didn't you get my note?'

'Yes. It made no sense to me. Did our time together mean nothing to you? I came back from Naros to find you gone, and there was no answer from the phone I gave you. Did you lose it, Eleanor?'

'No. I switched it off and bought a new one when I got home,' she said quietly.

His face hardened. 'To cut off all contact with me? Why?'

'Because, as I said in my note, it was time to get back to the real world and get on with my everyday life.' She coloured as her eyes fell from the penetrating black glare. 'I apologise. I deliberately gave you the wrong impression. I *am* a journalist, but not on a top London newspaper, Alex. I work on features in the *Chronicle* here in Pennington, and in between my travel articles I cover local events.'

'I knew that,' he said with scorn. 'I looked you up when I investigated Ross McLean.'

Of course he had. Eleanor sat down, feeling utterly stupid. 'Then now you can really see the difference between us. Your life revolves around Athens, London and even New York; whereas my trip to the Greek Islands was the most glamorous assignment I'd ever been given.' She looked up at him, unable to bear the suspense any longer. 'Have you come about the article?'

Alex sat beside her and took her hand. 'It was excellent, but I told you that before you sent it off.'

She looked down at their clasped hands, feeling her pulse accelerate at the contact. 'I didn't mean that one. There was a piece about your parents in another paper.'

'I have seen it.'

Eleanor raised her eyes in appeal. 'I didn't write it, Alex.'

'I know that! I knew you would not break your word, Eleanor.'

She almost fell apart with relief. 'Are you going to sue the paper?'

He smiled and raised her hand to kiss it. 'I was recently informed by a certain journalist that this would not be possible if the facts were correct. And, in this instance, they are. My parents are getting married again.'

Eleanor stared at him, astonished. 'Really? How do you feel about that?'

'My mother is so happy about it, I can only rejoice for her.' His eyes glittered. 'But I warned my father that if he hurts her again this time I will kill him.'

She grinned. 'Am I allowed to ask about his reply?'

'That is better,' he said in approval.

'What?'

'At last—you smiled at me!'

Her smile widened. 'Now tell me the rest!'

'My father assured me that he would willingly allow me to kill him in such circumstances, but that it would never happen, because he will devote the rest of his life to making my mother happy.' Alex shrugged. 'That is fair, *ne*?'

'I think it's wonderful. I liked your father.'

'He was most taken by you also, and called me all kinds of a fool for letting you get away.' He glowered at her. 'I was furious when I found my little bird had flown, Eleanor. My mood did not improve when my lady mother, who for some reason is convinced that I am madly in love with you, also called me certain names, of which "fool" is the most polite.'

'Are you in love with me?' demanded Eleanor.

He shook his head in disbelief. 'You think I chase halfway round the world for some other reason?'

'I thought you came to give me hell for breaking my word.'

'I knew you did not.'

'You trusted me?'

Alex gave her a wry smile. 'Of course I did, but I confess that Stefan contacted that rag to learn the name of the reporter.' His lips smothered the spluttering protest on hers with a kiss which took the fight out of her as he lifted her onto his lap without taking his mouth from hers, a move so familiar and spine-tingling she was lost.

'And you are in love with me, Eleanor,' he stated when he raised his head.

Her eyes flashed. 'Shouldn't that be a question?'

'I was ordered to give you this,' he said, ignoring her, and took an envelope from his pocket. 'It is an invitation to the wedding, which is to be small and private. My mother says you may simply be an honoured guest if you prefer, but you have her permission to report on the occasion and take photographs for your *Chronicle* if you wish. Your Mr McLean will like that, *ne?*'

She smiled happily 'He certainly will—but forget Ross. Which would you prefer, Alex?'

He gave her a quick, hard kiss. 'It is your choice, *kardia mou.* See how kind I am? I demand a reward for such kindness.'

'Oh, do you? What do you want?'

The dark eyes gleamed into hers. 'You are tired. There are circles under those beautiful eyes.'

'I haven't slept much since I saw you last,' she

admitted, and got to her feet, suddenly conscious that her hair was drying anyhow around a flushed face minus any make-up, and her fleece dressing-gown had been chosen for warmth rather than allure. 'As you can see, I wasn't expecting company tonight.'

'Since you are not dressed, I rejoice to hear it.' Alex got up to take her in his arms. 'I have not slept much either.' His eyes lit with familiar heat. 'I have a cure for this.'

Eleanor saw no point in coyness. 'If the cure involves a bed, I just happen to have a large one in my room. If you share it with me, perhaps we shall both get some sleep.'

Alex hugged her close. 'I can think of nothing I want more—except...'

'Except?'

'To make it clear that if we share a bed I will want more than sleep!'

She wriggled closer. 'I was rather counting on that.'

Much later, after a reunion so passionate it left them shaken and breathless in each other's arms, Alex said very sternly. 'Now we talk, *kyria*.'

'What about?' Eleanor asked dreamily.

'The future. These lives of ours that you believe are too different to join together—to me, the solution is simple. My life involves much travelling. You enjoy this, so you travel with me. As my lover, my partner; perhaps one day I can even persuade you to be my wife.'

Right now, if he liked. Every instinct urged her to say yes to anything he wanted, but Eleanor's inner realist hauled on the brakes. 'You'd have to convince me first.'

Alex smiled. 'Tell me how and I will do it.'

She turned it over in her mind, ignoring the impatience of his tightening arms. 'For the time being it's only sensible to carry on with our lives as they are, but for you to come to see me at regular intervals, here in the real world, as opposed to the adventure we shared on Kyrkiros.'

'If that is what you wish, I will do it, but not for long.' He pulled her higher in his arms. 'The only shadow on my parents' happiness right now is regret for all the years they wasted apart. They urge me not to repeat their mistake.'

'How about a year?'

He shook his head. 'Six weeks.'

'Six months.'

'*Three* months—no longer.' Alex put a stop to further haggling by kissing her. 'Tomorrow we visit your parents, *ne*?'

'I'm working tomorrow.' And Jane Markham would need some notice before her daughter sprang Alexei Drakos on her. Eleanor bit her lip. 'I should be working this weekend too, but I'll try and sort something. When do you leave?'

'I fly back on Monday, so tell McLean you need time off. Or I can tell him for you. We shall visit your parents on Saturday then drive down to Berkshire to mine on Sunday.' Alex smiled down into her startled face. 'This is how life will be, *glykia mou.* Does it change your mind about me?'

'Nothing could do that!'

'Then why in the name of Zeus are you making me wait so long?'

It was hard to think of a reason while Alex was kissing her again, but when he finally let her speak Eleanor told him the simple truth. 'I need to wait because this is still unreal to me, Alexei Drakos.'

'You need to be sure of your feelings before you commit yourself to me?' he demanded, frowning.

She took in a deep breath. 'No, Alex, I'm perfectly sure of my own feelings. I need to be sure of yours.'

His smile dazzled her. 'I love you, *kardia mou.*' He stopped dead, the smile suddenly crooked.

'What's wrong?'

'I have never said those words to a woman before.'

She grinned, secretly exultant. 'No wonder you looked so shocked.' She looked at him quizzically as he raised his eyebrows. 'Now what?'

'I am waiting,' he informed her.

'For what?' Though she knew.

'Tell me,' he commanded and pulled her hard against him. 'I will not let you go until you do.'

'Of course I love you, Alexei Drakos.' Eleanor smiled through sudden tears. 'But you can keep on holding me for a while, if you like.'

'For the rest of my life,' he assured her, kissed the tears away, then made her laugh by reaching for his phone. 'First ring down to your friend Pat to assure him I have not harmed you. Then we call your parents, after which we call mine, because my father is anxious for a sign that all is well between us. And then...' Alex paused, eyes glittering down into hers.

'And then?' she prompted, smiling radiantly.

'Before I go back to holding you, which will only lead to other things, I need food, *glykia mou*.' He grinned down at her. 'You shall display your cooking talents to me.'

'Ah, but what do I get in return?'

'Anything your heart desires but, with you here in my arms like this, I hope it is what my heart desires also.'

She grinned back at him. 'Or do you mean your body, Alexei Drakos?'

'Heart, soul and body,' he assured her. 'For as long as we both shall live.'

* * * * *